BARRY PARHAM

Blush

Politics and other unnatural acts

ISBN: 1453786198
ISBN-13: 9781453786192
Library of Congress Control Number: 2010912871

Also by BARRY PARHAM

Why I Hate Straws
An offbeat worldview of an offbeat world

Sorry, We Can't Use Funny

Kind Remarks From Some People Who Appear To Have Very Good Taste

"One of the funniest humor writers I've ever read, with a hilarious, sarcastic wit!"

"a delicious wit"

"This is just brilliant ... the kind of thing you want to keep close by and bring out for a good laugh."

"Barry will make you laugh aloud"

"There's nothing superior, judgmental or smug here, just an author who is massively enjoying himself and the net result is entirely infectious."

"a permanent item on my shelf"

"Hilarious, percipient, and so well written it could translate just as it is to stand-up comedy of a very sophisticated kind."

"reverentially irreverent, wry, dry and very funny"

"The prose is vibrant, punchy and as razor sharp as the wit"

"Wonderful, and you can't put it down until you're finished!"

"One of the funniest books I've read in a long time"

"brilliant ... a unique perspective on our everyday mundane world"

This book is dedicated to England's King George III

Were it not for his management skills,
we might never have thought to build
Washington, D.C.

—

A sad ending for what,
before politicians got involved,
had been a perfectly good swamp.

Table of Contents

Politics: The Gift That Keeps On Taking

Vote for Timmy!

(A new Manchurian Candidate courts the masses)

I'm building a politician, in case you're looking to buy one.

For a while there, I was thinking of running for office my-self. But I'm not going to lie to you. And there it is. If I can't lie to you, I'm not politically viable.

And then there's tact. Someone clever once defined 'tact' as the art of petting a dog while you reach for a sharp stick. Tact, I don't have. Tact, like 8-track tapes and velour, I gave up long ago.

So, instead of running for office myself, I'm building Timmy. Yes, Timmy. It's the least threatening name I could think of. (And given the current crop of sickos in Congress, I could hardly go with 'Lassie.')

Timmy is something new, something different. *Timmy is honest. Timmy makes sense.* On the down side, Timmy is an imaginary character, but if you look around at the current crop of options, well, WHY NOT? Democrats are too busy trying to reset their garden sundials for Daylight Savings Time. And Republicans are too busy asking for campaign contributions, so they can get re-elected, so they can fight for term limits.

So I'm building Timmy, and coding him for great things. We'll see how it goes.

Yeah, I know. In the highly-touted new Universal Health Care system, we're gonna have 200,000 fewer care-givers, but 30 million more care-demanders, and Washington plans to solve that piddling little mathematical anomaly in the obvious way: by hiring 16,000 more IRS agents. That, I can't fix.

Yeah, I know. You don't have a job, you can't afford a car, you can't afford a house, you don't want to live in public housing, and you can't afford to say 'God' in public. I can't fix that, either.

Yeah, I know. Life is tough, life is weird. Yeah, yeah, yeah. Whatever. Bunch o' whiners.

Look: I can't fix all that stuff. And neither can Timmy.

But I've coded Timmy with an alternative agenda that is guaranteed to please. Timmy will ease past the phenomenally huge things that are rending our delicate social fabric, and focus on grass-roots stuff: i.e., pet peeves. Timmy will address a laundry list of irritations that have been avoided for far too long. Witness:

Under the Timmy Administration, certain persons, groups, or things will be targeted for summary execution, unless we think of a more harsh penalty. And I bet we can. Like, say, eternal life spent in a north Georgia flea market, stuck between someone selling commemorative railroad plates and a pit-bull owner hawking free perfume samples.

Here's the current "These Things Must Go" list:

- Drivers who putt along in the left lane, treating it like their own personal kingdom, or who motor along for 1,800 consecutive miles with their left turn signal on, or who haven't yet figured out that their car is even equipped with a turn signal. Timmy may decide to just put all of these irritants in a giant bumper-car cage, charge admission, take bets, and delegate ultimate justice to Darwinian science.

- Senators who say that another Senator's activity is 'beneath the dignity of the Senate.' This is an especially vile travesty, and may require immediate intervention by the new Spanish Inquisition Czar.

- Phone message systems that helpfully remind you that 'when you're done, you can hang up'

- Drugs with a list of side-effects that are longer than the list of potential benefits. Punishment will be doubled if the side-effects include the word "leakage."

- Home security ads that claim that, during an actual emergency, they will really intervene in your on-going home invasion BEFORE you provide them with 28 super-secret security codes that you forgot long ago

- Appliance stores who sell you a clothes dryer that runs on electricity, and then charge you extra for the electrical cord

- Musicians who release 'Greatest Hits' albums that include one song you can't get anywhere else

- Hollywood pacifists who want to kick your butt because you won't sign their 'World Peace' petition

- People on Facebook who invite you to become a fan of things like the 'Eaton Hurl Diner & Bug Spray Museum, Located Just Off The Possum Colon Highway Spur In Lard Neck, Arkansas'

- People in the grocery's '10 Items Or Less' checkout lane who bicker for 28 minutes about their 4-cents-off coupon, or who appear utterly stymied at the concept of writing a personal check, as if the activity had never before been considered in the known universe

- Mexican restaurants that provide you with a fork that's been pounded flatter than Chernobyl real estate sales, and a knife that hasn't seen soap & water since Chichen Itza's gala grand opening (featuring Frank Sinatra singing 'Maya Way' and 'If I Only Had A Heart')

- Anyone who takes the time to answer a survey and responds 'no opinion'

- Anyone who uses 'impact' as a verb. If they use 'interface' as a verb, it will be considered a hate crime.

- Anyone who actually gets excited about an increased level of 'Bifidus Regularis' in their breakfast products

- Anyone who uses a badly-recorded version of Beethoven's Fifth Symphony as their cellphone ringtone. If they can't figure out how to turn off the ringtone, citizens have the right to immediately stone them.

- Anyone who says 'shoot me an email' or 'I just wanted to reach out to you.' If they invite you to 'interface,' you have the authority to spine-gas them on sight.

- Anyone who says with a straight face that Adam Sandler, in his last movie, made some 'interesting creative choices'

- Anyone who asks 'How much is your free membership?'

- Farmville. I need not say more.

So vote for Timmy! And stay tuned! In his second term, I'm gonna code him to understand the minds of network television programming executives.

Our Foundering Fathers

(A look back at Inauguration Day 2009)

What a day. Once again, America proudly witnessed another bloodless transition of power. Or blood transfusion of power. Or whatever it was. I forget. Anyway, nobody got hurt, and America will proudly witness stuff like that every chance it gets. The process worked, and power changed hands, and nobody got hurt. Maybe because it was too cold.

Days earlier, as the big event loomed, we were all glued to our television screens while professional, highly-paid, all-growed-up news pundits counted, and then re-counted, and then discussed, and then analyzed, and then interviewed the five-thousand-plus Port-O-Lets that would be hauled on to our National Mall. (It was a point of American pride that we had over 5,000 available toilets for an estimated 2 million visitors.) As one reporter pointed out, there were more toilets available than we have soldiers in Afghanistan. (I'm pretty sure that this reporter is also in charge of the return-on-investment analysis of our Wall Street bailout initiative.) Clearly not in the spirit of the thing, visiting superstar Madonna was overheard to say, "Pfhhh. 5,000 soldiers? *That* ain't a party."

The day started out on a bad note when outgoing Vice President Dick Cheney showed up. Yes, that IS, in and of itself, a pretty good joke. But I digress — The day started out on a bad note when outgoing Vice President Dick Cheney showed up in a wheelchair, having thrown out his back the previous night when someone at a college reunion party flushed a covey of quail. Though all the birds survived, the family members of Cheney's unfortunate graduating class announced that they would be receiving guests the following night at the Cheyenne Clandestine Memorial Chapel, from 8pm to 9pm.

A better tone was set when the incoming First Couple met the outgoing First Couple on the steps of the White House. There were hugs all round, and the incoming First Female Significant Other presented a gift to the outgoing First Female Significant Other. This kindness spurred the hovering photo-hounds into a frenzy of photo-hounding, until the Clintons leapt out of the First Shrubbery, stole the gift, and spirited it off to their First Legacy Museum. Bill Clinton then pardoned the shrubbery.

We got our first look at the new armour-reinforced Presidential limousine, which is supposedly able to withstand a direct meteor strike, or the first five minutes of a Wal-Mart sale, but not both. The limo, designed by General Motors, dropped an axle after it was nudged by a street hawker selling pictures of actual pieces of Obama's gardener's daughter's boyfriend's mother's ex-husband's mechanic. The pictures supposedly document an actual miracle, as they purportedly, every Christmas Eve, shed tears of real flex fuel.

The inauguration event itself was a true American memory. Attended by over 2 million Bank of America owners, it was a collective symphony of silly hats, including a lovely choice by Aretha Franklin, the incoming Secretary of Very High Notes, who seemed to have been cajoled into having a small game bird stapled to her forehead. Good thing Dick Cheney was busy not being available.

Around 11am, the Next First Official Motorcade And Way Long Bunch Of, Like, Motorcycle Cops And Stuff began the historic journey from the Linda Blair house to the site of the ceremonies. At least, I think it was the motorcade. All I really know for sure is that some helicopter was filming a bunch of cars going 2 miles an hour. For all I know, it could have been another O.J. car chase in L.A.

The motorcade proceeded apace and without incident, particularly since the motorcade route had been cleared of all traffic lights, curb-side trashcans, mailboxes, rude anti-anything cartoons, and crop circles that might attract eager Democrat-hating meteors. Even the manhole covers had been welded shut, which virtually ruled out any inter-ruptions by Japanese movie monsters violently exhaling beneath the streets, resulting in an eruption of O.J.'s origi-nal legal team.

Granted, it got even more weird when the Vice President-Elect began his oath with, "I, Joseph Hussein Biden…" But fortunately, sixteen hours into his oath, he was dope-slapped back into awareness by his lovely and talented wife, the first Vice Lady, Dr. Phil.

Even the Spare Change Messiah had a tough go, as he stood with his hand in the pocket of the Lincoln Bible, waiting to take the oath of office:

Chief Justice: I, Bara...no, wait...YOU, Barack Hu...no, wait...

Prez: My name. I got it. Move on, Chief.

Chief Justice: Will you faithfully uphold th...no, wait...will you hold up the faithfu...no, wait...will you fai...

Prez: And NOW you know why I opposed your nomination.

Things picked up a bit after the main ceremony when, during a luncheon, the keys to the White House vanished into a dimple on John Kerry's left cheek. Minutes later, upon discovering it was a cash bar, Ted Kennedy experienced a Major Medical Condition and had to be airlifted to the nearest T.G.I. Friday's. FAA officials are still searching for his engines, both of which fell into the Hudson River. And not to be outdone, Senator Robert Byrd, Strom Thurmond's paternal grandfather, also required medical attention after biting into his own dentures.

But as the day wound down, America remained safe. And confused. And broke. And cold.

And that, too, like everything else in history, apparently, is George Bush's fault.

Even now.

The 2010 Senseless

(Unlike us, Washington counts
their sheep BEFORE bedtime)

Here's the good news. Every ten years, we get to remind the government that we're still out here.

And here's the bad news. Every ten years, we remind the government that we're still out here.

If you're like me, you recently received your 2010 Census form. Well, that's not exactly accurate. Before you actually *received* your Census form, you probably received a massively expensive mailed piece *warning* you that were about to receive your 2010 Census form.

I used to have a friend like that. This friend would call me to say he wanted to drive over. Okay. Whatever. Then he would call again to say he was preparing to drive over, and then call yet again to tell me he was actually in the process of driving over. Occasionally, he would call me once more, from my own driveway, to tell me that he had managed to successfully drive over. This alert, apparently, was initiated so that I would have time to leap to the Sisyphean challenge of opening my front door, so he could stand inside my house and call me to let me know that he was standing inside my house.

I have a new set of friends now.

Our government is like that: you can't avoid their visit, they arrive and proceed to putz up your life and lifestyle, and then you can't get 'em to leave.

But shortly, as promised, the actual Census form arrived. Well, that's not exactly accurate. The crackerjack staff at the Census Bureau (Economic and Statistics Administration) sent me two identical Census forms.

Two. The counters sent two counting forms to one coun-tee. Not a good sign. This crowd can't even count to one.

And these are the people who intend to manage my medication and my body parts.

The Census form itself was delivered in a fat envelope bearing the big, bold warning that "YOUR RESPONSE IS REQUIRED BY LAW," which is always my preferred tactful tactic when I plan to ask people invasively personal questions about their private lives. Additionally, the envelope warned that there would be a $300 penalty if I attempted to use the useless thing for "private use." What "private use" would that be, exactly?

[Me] "Hey, Bill! Joey, across the street, checked 'Male' on his 2010 census!"

[Bill] "Thanks for the breaking news, Sherlock."

Inside the envelope, you're presented with a message from the Census Bureau Director, comfortingly assuring that your information cannot be used by the IRS, or any other highly-qualified medically-trained health care entity. However, you're warned that census data becomes public after 72 years, which means that after you're dead, people can find out that, 72 years earlier, you checked 'Male.' More importantly, the IRS may then immediately audit you for 72 years of pre-dead income, and require you to show up for a health audit, wearing nothing but an open-backed hospital gown and your checkbook.

After you've reviewed the cover letter and laid to rest your privacy concerns, it's time to deal with the Census form itself, which helpfully points out, at the top left of page one, that you should "Start here," in case you've never seen a form before, or you're a member of Congress.

You're then directed to count all people, including babies, who live and sleep at your address "most of the time," which puts old college roommates in a serious Census gray area (as I recall, a "gray area" is *exactly* where my old college roommates spent most of their time). Maybe that's who the "Start here" directive is for.

The multi-page Census form allows for data entry to let you list up to 12 people. Person 1 (that's you, Congressman) is asked to answer ten questions. Persons 2 through 6 have just seven to answer, and persons 7 through 12 have only five. If you have more than 12 persons living in your home, then you qualify for immediate reclassification as an idiot, unless you're Catholic or you're running a brothel (see ACORN addendum).

For each person, you must provide both their Age *and* their Date Of Birth, because calculating one from the other would require counting backward, and the Economics and Statistics Administration apparently forgot to hire any actual math majors. Each residing person is instructed to indicate their sex, and specifically instructed to only mark one box - which would boomerang me back to a discussion of my old college roommates, if I weren't busy filling out the Census form.

By the way, resident babies who are less than 1 year old are to be marked as age 0. As if it wasn't hard enough already to be an infant living in a brothel full of old college roommates. Which reminds me: you're not supposed to count people who are in jail, or prison, or college, or were sent to prison directly from college - and isn't it odd how my old college roommates keep showing up in this story?

One Census form topic I found overly interesting was "race." Among the available options are Black, White, Attorney, several flavors of Hispanic, Brothel, Unindicted College Roommate, Samoan, Hmong, Wall Street Broker, Tongan and Chamorro. I think they should've included Quaker.

No, really. I'm serious. Quaker. Stay with me here.

Recently, Quaker Oats redesigned the packaging for their "Chewy" breakfast bars, and by their own admission, the Chewy bars are now "exploding with goodness." I think it's important that you, as a duly double-counted American citizen, know about this. Breakfast is the most important meal of the day, unless it kills you. Nobody needs that much nutritional importance.

Ultimately, Team Census estimates that the average household will be able to complete the Census form in about 10 minutes, unless your household includes Wall Street Brokers or 0-year-old non-Male Samoans who sometimes sleep in Catholic prisons. And if you have any problems with this "burden estimate," you should scribble up a bunch of complaints and mail your paperwork to - ready? - the Paperwork Reduction Project.

Brilliant.

One more thing. Unlike you and me (remember: YOUR RESPONSE IS REQUIRED BY LAW), the staff at the Paperwork Reduction Project are not required to respond.

Well, not for 72 years.

Brussels Sprouts & Guillotines

(Your tax dollars at play)

Looking back, the trigger was easy to spot. The whole problem exploded when employees of the Securities & Exchange Commission were caught, during work hours, surfing the Internet for corn.

Understand, I'm hardly suggesting anybody could have predicted the resulting, culture-altering backlash, but you have to admit: the trigger *was* easy to spot.

Well-paid government employees, people who work for us, using computers purchased by us, spending their work-days staring at corn. And not just any run-of-the-mill, "non-essential" office gophers, either. These were the clever crew who, while the economy blew up, were supposed to be making sure the economy didn't blow up.

Meanwhile, mortgage foreclosures were heating up quicker than Sean Penn's temper. Retirement plans were shrinking faster than Larry King's ratings. Jobs were harder to find than a gay rights activist at a west Texas rodeo. And some guy named Madoff made off with the entire city of Boston.

And what were our watchdogs doing? Trolling the Internet for pictures of vegetables. J'accuse!

Not that there's anything intrinsically wrong with corn, mind you. I'm not here to judge, just to report. Some of my best friends like corn. But you don't bring it to work, for heaven's sake! You just don't.

And with this final outrage, Joe Six-Pack had finally had enough. The Iced Tea Party demanded accountability and threatened to wear more buttons. The entire nation was fed up. And Congress, smelling blood (and votes), did what Congress does best.

They over-reacted.

Rather than address the abuse, Congress attacked the availability. Typical, eh? If someone were to misuse a library book, Congress' solution would be to just close the library. Faced with outlaws on the streets, Congress would outlaw streets.

And so, in a rapid and rare bipartisan effort, Congress whipped up the 2010 Food Abuse Regulation Mandates: the FARM Act.

So here we are. A country without veggies. Criminalized corn and outlawed onions. A society sans sugar beets. One nation, under-dependent upon God, now self-banished from our own garden.

And so it began. A national task force was created, over-funded, and charged with policing Internet corn sites. At the state level, National Guard units were mobilized to padlock pole-bean-dancing clubs. The National Football League canceled their Super Bowl halftime highlighter, a popular band called The African-American-Eyed Peas. The Jolly Green Giant was hauled in front of a Senate commit-tee, who explained that though he wasn't technically guilty of a crime, he wasn't exactly helping matters by stomping around rural neighborhoods yelling "ho, ho, ho."

A Cotton Mather madness descended upon America. A lemming-like lunacy. In small towns across the heartland, city councils and ad hoc civic committees sprang into action, policing produce departments and scrutinizing school lunch menus. One activist, Mayor Torvald Armquist of Elk Blister, Nebraska, addressed the news media: "I don't know corn, but I know it when I see it." Fortunately, other activists heard him, and Armquist was immediately tack-led, heavily sedated, and whisked away for observation.

A reporter for The Times claimed to have proof that a Midwestern flight that had recently overshot its destina-tion airport was the result of pilots watching corn in the cockpit. Orville Redenbacher was arrested in Situ, South Dakota, and hung in Effigy, Iowa. And MSNBC claimed to have a compromising photo of Sarah Palin, but then they say that every week.

In one particularly conservative Wisconsin backwater, an alderman misread an evangelical tract, and as a result, mastication was declared a self-hate crime.

Farm subsidies skyrocketed, as farmers were paid more and more to grow less and less. As the news spread that farming now meant getting paid to not work, many career politicians abandoned their re-election campaigns, investing instead in a broad-brimmed hat and a pair of bib overalls.

As you might imagine, school kids were absolutely thrilled with this new "no more vegetables" national sentiment. Classrooms erupted in impromptu parades, and mock executions were held, during which various vegetables were beheaded. Brussels Sprouts, in particular, suffered greatly during these dark days.

Pro-produce groups were quick to challenge the new law. Willie Nelson, long an ardent farm supporter, called for a national boycott on beef, but was abducted by brisket-crazed patrons of a South Carolina barbecue chain. Coordinated chapters of the Future Farmers of America organized a huge hunker-in on the Washington Mall, at the Tomb of the Unknown Thresher.

Of course, we've learned nothing from history. If you tax something, you'll likely get less of it. And if you outlaw something, you'll likely get more of it. That's just the way people are wired. Once looking at corn was outlawed, black market produce markets started popping up on seedy inner-city side-streets. Geraldo Rivera hosted an investigative series on the rise of corn shops in Aruba. Cable networks capitalized on "grow-hibition" by rounding up B-list actresses and churning out low-budget, vegetably-suggestive movies with titles like "Maude Has A Salad" and "A Bell Pepper for Adano."

In Chicago, cleverly disguised "maize liquor taverns" sprang up overnight. All along the US-Mexico border, tortilla smuggling reached epidemic proportions. And a password-protected eBay channel took bids on thousands of poorly-lit produce photos before the channel was shut down by the Cornography Czar.

Eventually, things calmed down and we went back to our favorite TV shows. Nothing really changed.

And, not surprisingly, nothing really changed in Washington, either. Within a month of the FARM Act's passage, employees at Homeland Security were caught, during work hours, surfing the Internet for muslins.

Gods: 3, Chariots: 0

(Houston, we have a prodrome)

NOTE: This story should contain a warning. And since I wrote the story, it will.

WARNING: If, at this point in the ongoing grand rewiring of America, you're still a fan of President Obama, don't wait for the disclaimer. Just leave now.

DISCLAIMER: What follows is a lampoon of President Obama's recent speech at NASA. I downloaded the entire transcript from the Internet, which as we all know, contains zero errors.

SIDEBAR: I cannot guarantee that this story will contain zero errors, although it may contain the occasional author comment.

AUTHOR COMMENT: This is your final chance to leave now.

Thank you, everybody. (Applause) Thank you. (Applause) Thank you so much. (Applause) Thank you, everybody. (Applause) Please have a seat. Seat is spelled S-E-A-T. (Wild applause) Thank you.

You know, it's kind of humbling to stand here. (Derisive snorts) Here at NASA, very few people are impressed by Air Force One. (Laughter) Sure, it's comfortable, but it can't even reach low Earth orbit. (slide rules schussing, frantic scribbling, murmured algorithms)

Now, before I get to the part where I explain how I'm increasing NASA's budget by cutting NASA's budget, re-election protocols require me to say, at least once, that someone is "in the house." (Applause) I want to recognize Dr. Buzz Aldrin, who's in the house. (Applause) Where's Buzz? There he is. Buzz is in the house. (Applause) Four decades ago, according to my teleprompter, Buzz became a legend, like me, except I did it a whole lot quicker. Plus, I have a stunning profile, a professorial manner, and I often move my hands around like this. (Wild applause)

Your congresswoman, Anita Kosmos, is also in the house. (Scattered "who?" noises) Anita, who coincidentally happened to be on Air Force One during my flight down here today, voted for Obama-Care, which is a complete coincidence and has nothing to do with me being here today. Please give her a big round of votes. (Applause) I also want to thank everybody that wasn't specifically mentioned in my teleprompters, so please make a noise that sounds like "Applause" wrapped in parentheses. (Applause)

You know, it was from right here that the Hubble Telescope was sent into orbit, allowing us to plumb the deepest recesses of our galaxy, which saved or created 27 million Deep Recess Plumbing jobs. (Applause, mixed with Republican-sounding shouts of "you lie!")

I should point out, since it's an election year, that I have a picture from the Hubble hanging in "The Oval." So thank you for helping decorate my office. (Laughter) I should also point out my uncanny ability to take any topic, even the Hubble Telescope, and turn it into a discussion about me. (impressed sighs from egomaniacal politicians, who are in the house)

So here we have the story of NASA. It was here that men and women, propelled by sheer nerve, raw talent, and tons of coffee, set about pushing the boundaries of humanity's reach. And I looked around at it all, and I saw that it was good. (Scattered agnostic applause)

Over the years, NASA has contributed immeasurable technological advances, like Spandex, or whatever it is you guys do. As somebody said, "We're more than just Tang." Hey, I actually like Tang! (Polite laughter, overlaid with a justifiable "It's been 50 years; enough already with the lame Tang references" bitterness)

So today, I'd like to talk about the next chapter in this story. And let me start by being extremely clear. I am 100 percent committed to the mission of NASA. (Applause) Because you will serve our society in ways that we can scarcely imagine. Because exploration will inspire wonder in new generations. And because those new generations almost immediately forget anything I actually promise. So it's all good: I just keep promising stuff, then I move my hands around like this, and then I go play golf. (Applause)

I know there have been a number of questions raised about my administration's plan for space exploration, especially since my administration has no cogent plan for this or any other issue. So let me be clear. NASA was one of the areas in my budget where we didn't just maintain a freeze but we actually increased funding by $6 billion.

AUTHOR COMMENT: At this point, you may be feeling a bit queasy. As your guide, I'll give you a few moments to re-center yourselves. And I understand your confusion, because your instincts are correct. It is, in fact, not possible to freeze a budget and to increase it, too. I don't know what else to tell you. Breathe. Breathe. Okay, ready?

As a result of my kindness, we will probe the Sun's atmosphere. (Derisive snorts) We will plan missions to Mars. We will fund an advanced replacement telescope to replace the replaced Hubble, allowing us to peer deeper into space than ever before, so I can get a new picture to hang in The Oval. I've dubbed it the Double Hubble. (Sounds of several jaundiced guests leaving the room)

We will increase observation of Earth from space. In other words, we will fly out there and then turn around and stare at ourselves. And we will extend the life of the Space Station, while using it for its intended purpose: a purgatorial holding tank for conservative talk radio hosts.

Now, I recognize that some have said it is unfeasible or unwise to work with the private sector in this way. I agree. Because, when I'm done with this economy, there won't BE a private sector. Let's move on.

Next, we will invest more non-existent billions to design and build a deep-space rocket, no later than 2015. (Sounds of young NASA interns chanting and donning various Star Wars costumes) I have foretold such things in a vision, and decreed that they shall be invented, according to my schedule. (Swelling chanting noises)

The bottom line is that nobody is more committed to manned space flight than I am.

AUTHOR COMMENT: At this point, the lights in my office ominously dimmed. My computer keyboard actually stood up and stared at the transcript in disgust. It's true. At this point, even inanimate objects thought I was making this stuff up.

And so, by my 2025 coronation, my new spacecraft will take us into deep space. (Applause, mixed with sounds of interns checking their Facebook accounts) I've decided that we'll start by sending astronauts to an asteroid for the first time in history. (Uncontrollable snickering, inevitable "Bruce Willis" jokes) By the mid-2030s, early on a Tuesday, we'll send humans to Mars, or at least we'll send Joe Biden. And I expect to be around to see it. Because I am immortal. (Sounds of people paging themselves, so they can pretend they've just been summoned to an important meeting)

Now, some believe we should return to the Moon. But I just have to say pretty bluntly here: We've been there before. There's a lot more of space out there. (Collective "Well, DUH")

So we're going to modernize the Space Center and upgrade your launch facilities, which you must admit is very creative thinking, since you're about to lose all the funds you had to actually launch anything.

And there's potential for even more jobs as companies compete to be part of a new space industry. This holds the promise of generating more than 875 million jobs nation-wide by the end of next week. And many of these jobs will be created right here in Florida. I can guarantee that, because the White House is now in charge of the Census.

Now, it's true - there are conservative-leaning, non-union Floridians who will see their work on the shuttle end as the program winds down. And that's why I'm proposing another initiative, funded by taxpayers in other states, to create or save jobs right here in Florida. Call it 30, 40 trillion. Heck, 70. 80. Whatever.

Remember that these layoffs are based on a decision that was made six years ago, not six months ago, and I bring that up because I haven't used the word "inherited" in nearly eleven minutes.

Now, I'll close by addressing the question that some Americans have asked: Why spend money solving problems in space, when we don't lack for problems to solve here on the ground? And the answer is simple. Money's no problem. If I need more, I just print it. Whatever.

Little more than 40 years ago, astronauts descended the nine-rung ladder of the lunar module called Eagle, and allowed their feet to touch the dusty surface of the Earth's only Moon. They might have visited other moons, but in my wisdom, I only built one.

And the question for us now is whether that was the beginning of something or the end of something. I choose to believe it was only the beginning of the end of something. Or something. Whatever.

So thank me very much. I bless you. And may I continue to bless the United States of America.

(Sounds of several hundred rocket scientists logging on to Monster.com)

Pearls Before Pandemic

(How America's youth discovered a cure for Government Health Care)

Now that Congress has apparently graduated from Med School, they're putting their vast medical knowledge to good use, cobbling together 20,000 leagues of legislation to ensure we can all get sick for free, get dead when deemed best for the collective, and get buried under a bunch of new taxes.

We know the plan will work; after all, some real doctors dressed in white lab coats posed for a picture at the White House.

So far, so good.

On the down side, the bill, intended to insure everyone, doesn't. The bill, boasting to "bend the curve" of rising health care costs, can't. And the bill, promising to lower insurance premiums, won't.

On the plus side, nobody, including Congress, has read the bill. For all we know, it could guarantee free candy for all, and new teeth on demand.

So let's take a quick look at how they're managing their first health care issue: the flu.

DISCLAIMER: Nothing that follows is true. I hope.

December 2008

- World health panels predict a new strain of the Swine Flu. George Bush is blamed.
- The Center for Disease Control (CDC) admits they have no vaccines for a flu named after a farm animal.
- The White House admits they have no experience managing health crises (or, for that matter, anything else). But they do have unlimited funds with which to convert their fumblings into flawed public policy.
- Congress adjourns for the month.

January 2009

- The CDC determines that teenagers may need 2 different shots, administered in 2 different states.
- The Swine Czar consults political donors to see if anybody wants to become a supplier of vaccines and get very rich.
- Congress remembers that they forgot to include the flu in the Health Care Bill. They respond quickly, adjourning for a long weekend.

February 2009

- Vaccine contracts are awarded to a Chicago union shop that, naturally, makes hubcaps.
- The White House defends the decision diplomatically, stating, "You gotta problem with that?"

- The CDC confirms that teenagers will have to get 2 shots, especially if they've started dating. The hubcap union immediately strikes, demanding overtime.
- Obama insists that he inherited the Center for Disease Control from George Bush.
- Congress approves a new tax to print 350 million copies of "How To Sneeze Into Your Inner Elbow For Dummies."

March 2009

- The CDC updates its analysis, hoping that teenagers will only need 1 shot, unless they're really large teenagers.
- Congress discovers a typo in the Health Care Bill, resulting in $845 billion being allocated for something called the "Wine Flu."

April 2009

- The first case of Swine Flu is documented at a South Carolina pork barbecue. Witnesses say the victim had been trying to soul-kiss an unusually attractive, undercooked picnic shoulder.
- The CDC recommends that dating teenagers should enclose their hands in cement. Parents of dating teenagers heartily agree.
- The White House hints that the vaccines might be late. George Bush is blamed.

May 2009

- Across America, personalized surgical masks are all the rage. Fox debuts a new reality show, "Dancing With The Uninfected Stars."
- Wall Street brokers are encouraged, when closing "pork belly" business deals, to use the elbow bump.
- After an uptick in bank robberies, the FBI impounds all the surgical masks.
- Public schools are instructed to send students home if they notice any odd behaviour, like sneezing or being literate.

June 2009

- The White House admits that taxpayers paid for 325 million vaccines, but the hubcap union only delivered eight.
- Joe Biden advocates that Americans, particularly Republicans, stop exhaling, calling it "the patriotic thing to do."
- The CDC revises its revised revisions: teenagers will only need 1 shot, unless they've ever dated a farm animal.
- Congress announces an updated version of the Health Care bill. When asked about provisions for H1N1, Nancy Pelosi said, "The wha? ... Oh, shoot. Hang on."

July 2009

- Obama announces his new flu containment plan, declaring it the best plan he's come up with since the last plan he came up with, earlier that morning, before George Bush woke up.
- The CDC re-revises: teens may only require 1 shot, but their iPhone might require one, too.

August 2009

- Hillary reaches out to the virus for high-level summit talks, which sour immediately when she's introduced to the virus and asks, "Welcome to Washington, Your Flu-ness. May I call you 'Swine?'"
- Robert Gibbs bungles a briefing, calling the pandemic "H2N2," and the entire batch of vaccines gets scrapped.
- The CDC threatens that teenagers will have to get a whole bunch of shots, unless they agree to spy on their parents' tax returns.

September 2009

- Obama signs an executive order, mandating that only those earning more than $250,000 will get the flu.
- Independent sources release sobering statistics about the pandemic: more Americans have died from chopping garlic.
- The CDC guesses that teenagers might need a shot, or two, or more. They're just not sure, but they promise to Google it.

- Congress discovers another typo, and $687 billion is allocated to the treatment of "Spine Fluid."

October 2009

- During Halloween, Typhoid Mary masks are all the rage.

- For no apparent reason, Al Sharpton appears to make a public statement, but is swamped by people offering to buy his mask.
- The CDC re-calculates that dating teenagers need 3 shots. Parents of dating teenagers admit they need 3 shots, too. Of Scotch.

November 2009

- Obama blames the pandemic for low election turn-out. He signs an executive order, renaming it the "George Bush Flu."
- Poll-watchers invalidate some ballots that were cast by people who are actually dead. The ACLU logs a complaint, citing "post-oxygen bias."
- The Treasury offers to sell the CDC to Fiat.
- A calico cat in Texas contracts the flu. The ACLU logs a complaint, citing "anti-canine bias."
- Congress, clueless and critically close to a long week-end break, consults Stephen King about Captain Trips, and then earmarks $461 billion for "non-discretionary spooky stuff."

December 2009

- The CDC concedes that the shots won't work: all dating teenagers must be quarantined at Gitmo. Pre-Christmas iPhone sales plummet.
- The Ho-Ho-Ho Czar extends Christmas through the end of next March.
- The White House blames George Bush for flagging Christmas sales.
- The ACLU logs a complaint about the White House saying "Christmas."
- China offers to purchase Congress for fifty bucks. US citizens counter-offer, lowering the price to $29.95. Both sides do an elbow bump.

January 2010

- China ships Congress back to the US, citing intolerable defects.
- At Gitmo, teenagers are reclassified as aliens, as their parents always suspected. As aliens, the teens will be covered in the Health Care Bill.
- Due to an unforeseen outbreak of Ferret Flu, everyone in America dissolves into piles of thin brown dust, which is not covered in the Health Care Bill.

February 2010

- The Gitmo teenagers swim to Ft. Lauderdale for Spring Break, challenge China to a global game of Beer Ping-Pong, and win back all of America's debt.

And thus will America be saved, although the post-flu Congress will be full of hormone-raging, self-serving, immature brats.

So far, so good.

Welcome To The Machine

(Here's an idea: let's boil the politicians, and elect the sausage)

[Obama]   Well. Here we are. Distinguished guests, and Republicans, thanks for accepting my invitation to the Health Care Summit. As I've always said, I am confident that we will allow all sides to air their opinions and offer their suggestions, after which I'll head back to the office and sign the Health Care bill that I already wrote earlier this week.

Nancy Pelosi leaps to her feet.

[Nancy Pelosi] Meeting adjourned!

[Obama] Easy, girl. Okay. Before we get started, I'd like to make some brief opening remarks, since there are cameras in here. As I've always said ...

48 minutes later …

[Obama]   ... and that's why, as I've always said, make no mistake.

Pelosi leaps to her feet.

[Pelosi] Yay! Yay!

[Obama] Okay. Let me be transparent and toss out a bipartisan bone. Let's hear from the Minority Whip. Senator McConnell?

[Mitch McConnell] Thank you, Mr. President, but I'm not the Whip. I'm the Minority Lea...

[Obama] Hold up, Mitch. Hey! Fox News! Can you guys hear us okay back there?

[Small Voice At The Back Of The Room] Hey, this outlet's dead!

[Obama] Whatever. Hit it, Whip.

[McConnell] Thank you, Mr. President. I yield to my distinguished colleague, our Minority Leader, Mr. Boehner.

[John Boehner] Thank you, Senator. I yield to my distinguished colleague, Senator Alexander.

[Lamar Alexander] Thank you, John. I yield to my distinguished colleague, who also happens to be a respected doctor.

[Respected Doctor] Thank you, Senator. Mr. President, if you'll take a look at this chart, you'll clearly see tha...

A buzzer sounds.

[Obama] Okay, that's your side's turn. Thanks for your valuable input. Speaker Pelosi, would you like to say a few words while you're in my presence?

[Pelosi] I'm not worthy.

[Obama]   True enough. How 'bout our Majority Leader, then? Senator Reid? *HARRY*!

Harry Reid snaps out of his light snooze, spins around, and addresses the wall behind him.

[Reid] I have, here in my hand, a let...

[Obama] *Whee-eew-eet!* Over here, Sparky.

Pelosi gyros Reid's chair back to front. Harry blinks several times, waves at the assembled crowd, and then finds his place.

[Reid] I have, here in my hand, a letter I'm holding here in my hand from a Nevada resident, Michael Lattoral, a simple, hard-working citizen from Nevada. Michael is supporting his mother, an illegal alien who lost the left side of her face in a poorly-planned card trick. And then Michael lost his job and had to start beating his wife. As a result of these tragedies, and several niggling arrest warrants, they have no insurance as a result. And that's why I say we have to act now! I don't how to make it any more clear than that clear.

[Respected Doctor] As this chart on spousal abuse shows, there is no clear correla...

[Obama] You know, every day I get 20 million letters from Americans, and my staff picks out about a dozen of 'em for me to read, or so I'm told. Make no mistake - those letters deserve better. And that's why, as I've always said, I'm signing an executive order which will save or create 20 million jobs, opening letters.

Pelosi leaps to her feet.

[Pelosi] You're just too good for us, sir.

[Chris Dodd] Union jobs, right?

[Obama] And heading up this new initiative will be my good friend and partner, Vice President Jim Biden. 'Cause nobody messes with Jim.

[Joe Biden] It's *Joe*, sir. *Joe* Biden.

[Obama] Whatever.

[Respected Doctor] Mr. President, I have another chart here that I think will help clear u...

[Obama] Give it a rest, Sawbones.

[Reid] What's that noise?

A minor demon materializes, points to a yellowed contract, and swallows Chris Dodd.

[John McCain] Looks like Chris gets letters, too.

[Obama] Say what? Sorry, John, didn't hear you. I was looking over the election results. Seen 'em yet?

McCain stares at a point in the near distance, grinding his teeth.

[McConnell] You know, I have a letter here from one of my constituents, Eaton Krill. Mr. Krill's insurance was canceled after he was diagnosed with recurring neck bolts. And that's why we need to scrap this whole bill and start over.

[Obama] Make no mistake. As I've always said, we don't have time to start over. We've spent hours in here already, and there's no way I'm keeping this tie on much longer.

[Pelosi] It's a lovely tie, sir.

[Lamar Alexander] I have some letters with me, too. Does anybody want t...

A buzzer sounds.

[Obama] MY TURN!

Pelosi leaps to her feet and clamps a rose between her teeth.

[Obama] No, not *that* "my turn," Nancy.

[Reid] Sir, that one's me. It's time for my medication.

[Respected Doctor] You know, speaking of medication, I have a chart here that I'm sure w...

[Obama] Okay, let's see. According to my watch, it's time for me to look around the room, nodding in a bipartisan way, while staring at a point in the near distance and effecting a concerned yet controlled frown.

[Pelosi] Yay! Yay!

[Obama] Imagine it, John. Millions of letters. Every day. Hey, John, how many letters *YOU* gettin' lately?

[McCain] Sir, I'm not sure how that's relevant to this discu...

[Obama] Okay, John. Enough of your petty partisan bickering. The election's over, John. I won.

McCain hurls a pencil, pinning a CNN reporter to the wall.

[Obama] Hey, John! I. Am. The. President.

Nancy Pelosi falls to the floor, swooning.

[Obama] Hey, Sawbones. Revive the chirp, wouldja?

[Respected Doctor] Revive *this*.

Progress or Congress?

(Eco Cars, Wacko Czars and
Capitol Stars: beware the Axis of Stupid)

We've heard about all the new Czars: the Car Czar, the Energy Czar, the Green Czar, the Lime-Green Czar, the Cola Czar, the Diet Cola Czar, the Cola With Just A Hint Of Lime Czar, the Bee-Czar, the Czar In Charge Of Forest-Dwelling Quadrupeds Under Eighteen Inches In Height.

But we only just learned that over 200 "normal" administration positions are still unfilled. Minor jobs, to be sure, like head of the DEA, half the Treasury, and Midnight Intern Pizza Delivery Coordinator. But still.

More disturbing, these 3 or 4 dozen Czars are running around, Czaring all over the place, without any Senate approval - despite a clear admonition from our Founders who, in their wisdom, foresaw some future, out-of-control President attempting to self-appoint shady characters that seem to have been drawn from foreign novels.

According to my copy of "The American Constitution As Originally Bunged Together By Several Guys Wearing Wigs And Knickers," and I quote: *If any jerk ever starts appointing Russian rulers, he shall be duly told to 'knock it off.' Then shall his Virginia-sized ego be forcibly removed and converted into a public park.*

So I was glad when the President recently nominated somebody for a Cabinet position; glad that, for a change, the Senate would get to do something that was actually legal.

Hurrying home to watch the confirmation hearings, I spotted this oddly-shaped lime-green blob, throbbing along in the lane ahead of me. It looked like a car, almost, but smaller; maybe a car left in the dryer too long; maybe a car digitally morphed by movie software.

It looked like a car cartoon.

The thing was dabbling forward at a blistering 30 miles per month, so I coasted alongside to get a closer look. Ah. It was the debut effort from Government Motors. The plastic-baked, eco-friendly, hilariously silly-looking car of the future.

It was the *Obama Smote*.

The Smote looked like a prank pulled off by some deranged lumberjack, who took a real car from Earth, lopped off everything except the front seat, and then glued on headlights and taillights. And the driver looked like somebody who had lost a frat-house bet. There was barely enough room in the car's cabin for the owner's *manual*, much less the owner.

The driver wore that taut expression often exhibited by out-patients when undergoing certain highly personal and invasive cleansing procedures. The pretzel-sized steering wheel was shoehorned against his chest. He had undoubtedly left his legs at home. No way they would've fit in the car. Or, for that matter, the trunk.

A few yards along, he somehow activated his turn signal. The electrical surge blew out his headlights, and the turn-signal wand slashed through the door and punctured his front tire.

At home, the Senate hearings on TV left much to be desired. Eleven hours after they convened, the Cabinet nominee pre-resigned, stormed out, and took a part-time job baking Smotes. The assembled Senators didn't notice, as they were still spouting their opening misstatements.

[Harry Reid] If there's no objection, I'll now dispense with all history, logic, and common sense.

[Arlen Specter] I heartily approve of these bipartisan proceedings, and I heartily disapprove, too.

[Chuck Schumer] My distinguished colleague straddling both sides of the aisle can go spit.

[Arlen Specter] Aw, go rent out your face, Forehead Boy.

[John Kerry] Apres moi, le deluge.

There was a knock on the chamber door.

[Nancy Pelosi] Excuse me. Does 'swastika' have two K's or three?

[Harry Reid] Senators, Nancy! For the last time! Senators Only! Get out, woman.

[Barbara Boxer] I worked hard not to be a woman.

[Lindsay Graham] Don't fight it, Toots.

A cloud of ironed hair boils in through the side door, closely followed by Chris Dodd.

[Chris Dodd] Sorry I'm late. I ran over a Smote.

More Stockholm, Less Syndrome

(Some thoughts on bogus
prizes, real czars, and blowing stuff up)

Stockholm, 1833. Alfred Nobel was born. He would go on to create Peace Prizes ... *and* dynamite. And I'm spending the day searching world history for an irony bigger than *that* one. Wish me luck.

I bring this to your attention because, in a surprise proclamation from Stockholm, our fledgling President was just awarded the Nobel Peace Prize.

I'm not kidding. The Nobel Peace Prize. Awarded to a man who's had less experience brokering peace than a Woodstock t-shirt vendor.

Now, don't get me wrong. I don't begrudge our President's being publicly lauded by Europe; after all, he's doing his best to bring America into the European Union. And he is a card-carrying, thunderbolt-wielding member of the Olympian Pantheon.

Plus, not even Chicago backroom politics could put the fix on the Nobel Prize Committee, right? Could they? I'm sure it's pure coincidence that, days before the vote, Nobel voter Sven Bidetplungger woke up next to the misplaced head of his horse.

No, our President has justly earned the Nobel Peace Prize, for reasons I will document herein.

Alfred Nobel was the son of a Swedish businessman, named Alfred's Father, who went bankrupt at least twice. Apparently, he couldn't manage to turn a profit *providing military supplies to military-supply-hungry Czars*, which then and now makes for a pretty lame résumé.

[Nobel Justification Update: our President can't seem to manage the managers of the wars his managers say he's managing. But he's doing a crackerjack job at going bankrupt.]

When Alfred's dad wasn't busy being hounded by half-staffed Czars, he built bridges. And in a delicious twist of fate, Alfred's career would turn to finding some substance he could use to blow stuff up: stuff like, say, his dad's bridges.

One Christmas, Alfred, while still a Swede-ling, received a gift from his mother (named Alfred's Father's Wife) that would change history: "My First Detonation Kit," which she picked up at Waal-Marknaden for under 12 kronor (batteries and appendage bandages not included). And a career was born.

[Nobel Justification Update: our President plans to pre-approve your toys, grant you green batteries, and mete out government-issued band-aids. And though he was never a Swede-ling, he apparently has some experience with "swaddling."]

A glimpse into young Alfred's potential materialized early on, when a hasty experiment involving nitroglycerin blew some stuff up, including his brother (named Eric, but not for long), along with several members of Alfred's après-school Arts and Crafts club.

History tells us that Alfred's Father was worried about his son's tendency toward introversion, so he sent Alfred abroad to spend some quality time in the company of career chemical engineers. I'm sure that many of you with socially-cautious children have considered the same therapeutic approach. Nothing like clabbering with a clutch of cloistered chemists to tease out that dormant man-about-town gene, eh?

[Nobel Justification Update: our President has some interesting "citizen modeling" plans for *your* kids, too!]

But eventually, as we all know, Alfred invented dynamite, a very stable way for unstable people to blow stuff up. Students of irony will note that dynamite became an instant favorite of peace-lovers everywhere, and also netted Alfred about 483 bungostillion dollars, or about half of America's current debt, not counting interest, health care, the military's need to blow stuff up, and next week's surprises.

And all of Alfred's wealth led to the funding of the famous Nobel Prizes. And all of this leads us back to the fact that our President just won one.

Let's review some other Nobel laureates:

Charles Kao, for "groundbreaking achievements concerning the transmission of light in fibers for optical communication."

Carol Greider, for "the discovery of how chromosomes are protected by telomeres." As if we all didn't already know *that* about telomeres. Phhh.

Venkatraman Ramakrishnan (and others), for "studies of the structure and function of the ribosome." Sadly for VR, top billing went to Thomas Steitz, since his name would fit on the little commemorative coins.

George "Dubya" Bush nearly won once, in the Physics category, for his brilliantly deductive leap: "imports come from overseas." But he was edged out by a real poser, presented by the US Post Office: "if it's under 70 pounds, you don't have to weigh it." As we speak, several hundred abstract physicists with corduroy elbow patches are pondering this little Schrodinger's Catnip: How does one know it's under 70 pounds until one weighs it?

And now, our President has won a Nobel Peace Prize for, as best as I can tell, "groundbreaking achievements concerning the transmission of hope in tandem teleprompter communication." I understand he's also the odds-on favorite for the Heisman Trophy and Woman Of The Year.

Upon hearing about his award, during a taxpayer-funded Air Force One lunch commute to a Chicago Taco Bell, our modest President read a poignant speech. He read about how humbled he was to be the only Olympian God ever to win a Nobel Prize. He read that he was honored to hang out with such an august assemblage, since most of his earlier friends also liked to blow stuff up, or were irreverent reverends, or sported catchy monikers like Tony Two-Fingers and Mick The Nose.

White House Voice-Organ Robert Gibbs said, "Obviously, we obviously didn't expect this, but obviously, we, uh, to the end and, did they not? But I obviously don't want to get into theoreticals here, so, and they do might, well, um."

And so, let's close with a telling quote from Alfred himself:

"Second to agriculture, humbug is the biggest industry of our age."

Well met, Alfred.

Well met.

Mannequin of the People

(How much is that politician in the window?)

This week, I got a piece of mail urging me to consider voting for a certain candidate. It was the most honest political tract I've ever read, which I admit isn't saying much. Granted, given your average political tract, the letter did not exactly rise to a "Breakthroughs In American Literature" moment. But I was impressed.

Actually, I got no such thing in the mail. But you surely know by now that I'll flick off truth like a bad hat. I never let truth get in the way of a good story. Plus, we're talking about politics here, so lying can't be far behind.

So here's the letter. Trust me.

-~-~-~-~-

Dear Concerned Citizen,

I'm writing to ask for your vote.

My name is unimportant. After all, I'm just one more faceless drone in a sea of opportunists who have made a career out of making a career out of your money.

But you may recognize me as the well-dressed wax dummy in the store window down at Fred Knott's Big 'N' Tall Gents.

You all know Fred and his store: "Want a fair deal? Fred Knott!"

For those who don't know me, my name is Jerry Mander. I'm married to the lovely Sally Mander, and we have two adopted sons, Eft and Newt Gingrich, fine lads with no pending indictments. Our children are enrolled in public or private schools, depending on polls, and we attend the same church as you, whichever church that is.

Trust me.

For decades, I've stood in Fred's window, doing whatever my handlers tell me to do - posing, participating in staged success stories - and always with an extended, upturned palm, posturing for some more of your money. I have perfect hair, perfect posture, a purchased smile, and free clothes. I can change positions faster than Arlen Specter.

I can be whatever you want me to be: tall or short, dark-skinned or fair, a paragon of success, a tabloid trash-item, a societal blister. I'll provide young people with what they want and protect old folks from what they fear. I can fake being glib, firm, thoughtful, pensive, or elated ... whatever my handlers tell me is wanted that day.

I've never done anything in my entire life except stand around in public with my hand out, offering unfounded allure and promises to passersby. And the way I figure it, that qualifies me to run for public office.

I'm at least as qualified as any of the malleable bipeds and sycophantic sock puppets you people keep re-elect-ing now - and I'm much better groomed. Chris Dodd, for example, looks like he's auditioning to play Sting's father in a "Dune" remake.

So where do I stand on the issues?

Health Care: I've not actually read it, but our proposed plan is without doubt the best plan we've come up with since the last plan we came up with, sometime earlier today. Haven't read that one, either.

The Global War on Overseas Contingency Operations: Nothing is more critical than national security, and that's why I heartily agree with our President that we shouldn't be listening to decorated Generals, in-country soldiers, and in-the-know intelligence experts. Rather, we should take our military cues from John "Chin-Bayonet" Kerry, who bravely lobs unarmed medals at defenseless fences, and ace military expert Joe Biden, who couldn't leak more if he was a crab trap.

Taxes: I am firmly on record as being absent for any votes on tax increases, though I sponsored most of the bills. I do, however, remain open to revenue enhancements, tariffs, fees, set-asides, mandates, alternative funding, ancillary monetary inducements, budget shortfall compensations, upward adjustments in participatory contributions, wallet extractions, and vital investments for our future. We're only doing it for you, you know.

So, this November, I'll be asking for your vote, and today, I'll begin asking for your money. Please consider making a contribution to my campaign. I understand that times are tough. Believe me, I get it. As one of my heroes once said, "I feel your pain."

If not for me, do it for my hero. Wasn't he just the best ever? Amazing. Empathetically biting his lip, while simultaneously nibbling your ear. And you guys still love him, too. I know.

How do I know? Polls. People like me won't even generate insulin without first taking a poll.

In one recent poll, 24% responded that they had no opinion. Imagine it. People took the time to respond to an Opinion Poll, just to admit that they didn't have an opinion.

And they call *me* a dummy.

So send me money. The more money you send me, the less of your pain I'll feel.

Trust me.

Anybody Else Will Do

(Everybody hates Congress. But everybody loves their member of Congress. This could get tricky.)

Congress is broken.

It no longer works, and they definitely no longer work for us. So let's just send them home.

ALL of them. Every single one. Thanks very much, Congress, but we'd like to try somebody else. You're just not cutting it. Go home.

Welcome to "Anybody Else Will Do," an grass-to-astro-turf-roots mob of stupid, rude, raving maniacs who seem oddly intent on preserving the American dream and preventing all this cradle-robbing-to-grave-robbing control by an utterly out-of-control, out-of-touch government.

Citizens: It's been tried before. Let's try it again. All you have to do is vote ... for ANYBODY ELSE.

Congress: Enough already. You rarely even do any actual work. And when you DO work, it's worse.

Listen. We don't want you to dictate how much water our toilets can flush. We don't want you to hold America's national security hostage by ignoring our borders, or by slipping personal pork projects into our defense budget.

Listen. We don't all want to pay for one state's "vital" Solar-Powered Peanut Storage Research Center. We don't want a formerly-honored federal institution to spend days crafting a non-binding resolution to commend some football team for winning the Orange Bowl.

We don't want you to control the acceptable amount of rodent hairs found in food products. (Actually, we believe the acceptable amount of rodent hairs is zero, or, if possible, less.)

You stole our money from Medicare. You stole our money from Social Security. And then you voted yourselves a raise. Several times. At night.

You managed to lose money running a *casino*. You managed to lose money running Amtrak and the Post Office, and those were **MONOPOLIES**. The Post Office is the only "business" on earth that can raise prices when business goes **down**.

And now you expect us to let you manage our global battlefields? Our health care? Get out. You can't even manage a used car swap.

We don't want you to control our lives, our incomes, our habits, our education, our religion, our children.

We want our control BACK.

Congress. Out-of-touch, out-of-control, self-serving? Negligent, dishonest, overpaid? Definitely.

Untouchable? No.

Enough already.

Here at Anybody Else Will Do, we use a little decoder to differentiate between what politicians say and what they really mean. For example:

When they say:
I sincerely believe...

What they really mean is:
According to a new poll...

See how it works? Pretty handy, eh? Here are some more helpful decodings:

At the end of the day...
Here comes my spin on the subject.

The truth of the matter is...
Here comes my party's spin on the subject.

But where the rubber hits the road...
Here comes my PAC's spin on the subject.

Let's take a step back...
I can answer that, or I can keep my job.

Obviously, our plan was...
Man. Did we ever foul up THAT one.

My distinguished colleague...
That pig...

While I have the greatest respect for...
That pig is holding up my bill.

We're very close to a vote...
That pig is holding up my bill for more pork.

We had broad bi-partisan support...
It was sweet! The entire committee was for sale.

My friend on the other side of the aisle...
That pig is SO not getting on this committee.

It all boils down to a matter of opinion...
That pig's not here, is he?

That quote was taken out of context...
I was lying.

I can categorically state...
Nobody can prove I was lying.

In all fairness...
Nobody can prove I was lying about lying.

That is unequivocally false...
I was lying, but it hasn't leaked yet.

Let me say for the record...
Here comes a brand new lie.

We're not going to get into hypotheticals...
Yeah, that's exactly what we did. Or will do. Probably. Or not.

Believe me when I tell you...
HA HA HA HA HA HA HA HA!

What the American people really want...
What I really want...

On behalf of my constituents...
I'm in a tough re-election campaign.

It's an unfunded mandate...
Your paycheck's about to get jacked. Again.

I did not have sex with that woman...
I had sex with that woman.

Enough already.

Anybody else will do.

Tubular Gerbil Insurance

(If it's really gonna be UNIVERSAL
health care, let's include snakes)

Are you one of those people who think snakes are fun? One of those people who think snakes are cool, and make great pets? You are? Did you know you are bat-scrabbling insane?

I've always been afraid of snakes. And I don't mean "afraid" in the traditional sense, the cute, endearing, "oh, he'll grow out of it" way. I'm talking about something primal, something genetic. When I was still a tiny little humor-column-writing mitochondria, I caught a glimpse of my double helix and ran away, in a cute, not-yet-having-developed-legs kind of way, burbling "SNAKES!"

So my fears formed long ago; so long ago, in fact, that when a pre-natal scan of my humor-column-writing fetus disclosed that I was afraid of snakes, there were only 28 million Americans without health insurance. See? Way, way back.

When it comes to snake-o-phobia, I've got it bad. In the delivery room, at the moment of my birth, I hid behind my mother's lungs and tried to kill my own umbilical cord with a hoe.

[Historical Sidebar: at the moment of my birth, there were only 44 million Americans without health insurance.]

Psychoanalysis aside, I come by my phobia honestly. At age 12, I was a proud Boy Scout in an America that had only 92 million citizens without health insurance. One bright weekend morning, our troop was dutifully collecting roadside litter and dirty jokes, jokes that inevitably involved that versatile verb-slash-noun, "poot."

As I clawed into the rough brush for another handful of roadside refuse, a conscientious snake, obviously concerned about the growing problem of uninsured Americans, leapt at my face in an apparent effort to reduce the national tally by one. My face responded by planting itself about 9 inches deep in the thigh of the nearest fellow Scout, who was, by my reckoning, some 14 feet to the east. It was, truly, a leap for the record books.

That day, I made it home alive. I was older, wiser, and badly in need of some Boy Scout-approved hiking shorts cleaning fluid.

Time passed, and I entered the Age Of Orthodontics, that privileged period of puberty marked by the appearance of a wicked, white-coated stranger, straight out of the Spanish Inquisition, who actually got paid by my parents to fill my mouth with sharp metal rings and evil tightening screws.

[Historical Sidebar: during the Spanish Inquisition, there were only 6 Americans without health insurance. Of course, without the comfort and surety of government-run health care, they all died. Eventually.]

So, one day, when there were only 148 million uninsured Americans, my mother and I were preparing to visit the

Ortho-demon. Spry, young, and immortal, I popped out the back door, hopped over the wrought-iron railing, and nimbly landed on the floor of the garage ... right next to a coiled copperhead snake.

As there were no nearby Boy Scout thighs, I opted for a Ringling Brothers-style leap, flat-footed, from the garage floor to the hood of my mom's car. The snake actually applauded. I, playing it safe, accepted the duties of family sedan hood ornament, where I remained until my parents agreed to park somewhere else.

I haven't been back home since. For all I know, the snake is still in the garage.

And then yesterday, I heard two disturbing stories on the news. Firstly, Florida wildlife officials are concerned that escaped pet African Rock Pythons and escaped pet Burmese Pythons may be mating in the wild, after drinking too much at Escaped Pet Happy Hour, destined to create some kind of escaped pet Super Snake. PETA has already filed a suit, demanding mutant snake health insurance.

[Historical Sidebar: if you don't think there's such a thing as Escaped Pet Happy Hour, then you obviously don't know much about Florida.]

And secondly, I heard that there are now more uninsured Americans than there are Americans. Apparently, some of them are so pitifully uninsured that we're counting them twice.

But in the spirit of creative marketing, as exhibited by government statistics on uninsured Americans, let's give the snakes a break. Going forward, let's not call them snakes. Let's go with something less threatening, something more marketing-friendly. Let's call them tubular gerbils.

If you're interested, contact Florida wildlife management. Contact them before happy hour.

But buy one now, while you're still insured.

Bob's Last Day

(Bully pulpits, citizens' arrests, and corporate corporal punishment)

911: 9-1-1. What is the nature of your emergency?

Caller: I think I just witnessed a murder!

911: What is your current location?

Caller: I'm at home, in front of the TV.

911: You witnessed a murder there, in your house?

Caller: No, on TV!

911: Ma'am, it's a serious offense to make prank calls t...

Caller: It's *not* a prank!

911: Your name, please.

Caller: My name? My name is Liberty. Miss Liberty. My friends call me "Belle." Please help!

911: Okay, please calm down, ma'am.

Caller: But I think I just witnessed a murder!

911: Ma'am, I still don't understa...

Caller: I was watching the State of the Union address, and I think I saw the Constitution get murdered!

911: Ah, that. Yes, ma'am, we've gotten several calls about that already. I assure you that the Constitution is alive and well. For now.

Caller: You're sure? It looked so *REAL*!

911: I understand. I heard it got pretty bloody.

Caller: Oh, it was *awful*! The President attacked the Supreme Court! He said tha...

911: (aside) *Hey, Bob. Pick up. This one's a keeper.*

Caller: What?

911: Nothing, nothing. Just a standard internal 9-1-1 procedure. Please go on.

Caller: He insulted the Supreme Court Justices!

911: Th ... the *Supreme Court*? One of the co-equal branches of government?

Caller: Yes! Right there, in front of Himself and everybody!

911: Hold on. The President stood there, on national television, and said the Supreme Court had "acted stupidly?"

Caller: Hmm. That sounds familiar.

911: (aside) *Bob, buzz Dispatch. We may have a Pending Beer Summit Alert.*

Caller: And then he fibbed about a Supreme Court decision!

Bob: You don't say! A politician, lying. Hang on - I'll alert the media.

911: (aside) *Cut it out, Bob.*

Caller: And it wasn't just incompetence, either. The President *knew* it wasn't true!

911: Now, how do you know that?

Caller: Because he was reading from a teleprompter! Two of them!

Bob: Maybe George Bush snuck in and changed the teleprompter copy.

911: (aside) *WHACK!*

Caller: What was that?

911: Nothing, nothing. By the way, can you help us confirm a previous caller's statement?

Caller: I, uh, I can try.

911: Someone else phoned in a report that Speaker of the House, Nancy Pelosi, might be involved in narcotics trafficking.

Caller: No!

911: Well, apparently, the Speaker was observed having some kind of involuntary spasms. Leaping out of her seat, several dozen times during the speech. Stuff like that.

Caller: You know, you're right! She did do that. Plus, she parachuted into the room and pole-vaulted to the podium.

Bob: Oh! Oh, I can't breathe.

911: (aside) *Bob...*

Caller: And now that you mention it - at one point during the speech, an aide in a loud red dress handed her a little white packet. I thought it was just a note!

Bob: And then there's that weird, Salvador Dali droopy-face thing going on, too.

911: (aside) *WHACK!*

Bob: (aside) *Wha-ha-ha-t?? What'd I say?*

Caller: Actually, a lot of the Congresswomen showed up wearing pretty loud outfits. When the camera panned the crowd, the place looked like a bag of Peanut M&Ms.

911: Can't help you there, ma'am.

Caller: Come to think of it, Joe Biden looked pretty wired on something, too. All that clenched-jaw grinning. All that pouty, professorial nodding. All those teeth!

911: We'll look into it. Any other observations about the alleged murder?

Caller: No, I don't think there wa ... oh, wait! I almost forgot!

911: Go ahead?

Caller: The President spoke about some bill that Congress had just refused to sign.

911: As well he might. And?

Caller: Well, then the President said it didn't matter. It didn't even matter what Congress did! He said he would just sign an executive order, and do what he wanted anyway!

911: He. Did. Not.

Caller: He did! I saw it!

911: The President blew off the *other* co-equal branch of government, too?

Caller: See? It's murder! The Constitution is dead!

911: Calm down, ma'am.

Caller: But the Constitu...

911: It's gonna be fine, ma'am. I assure you. The Constitution has survived much worse than this.

Caller: But can't we do *something*? Can we sue somebody? Can you find me a lawyer?

Bob: Phht. *Can we find you a lawyer?* In *America?* Are you *kidding me?* Ever seen a phone book? Ads for attorneys on the front cover, back cover, inside covers, and those little tabbed pull-out page thingies. Not to mention all those fridge magnets.

911: (aside) *Bob, I've just abou...*

Caller: And then, after the State of the Union speech, the President flew off to Florida to announce an $8 billion bullet train, to help people not get to the jobs they don't have, really fast.

911: Whew. You're right - this guy is out of control. Okay, ma'am. We'll send out a SWAT van to pick him up.

Bob: Two vans.

911: (aside) *Bob...*

Caller: Two?

911: (aside) *Bob, don't do it...*

Bob: Yeah. One for him, one for his ego.

911: (aside) *WHACK!*

Wring Out The Old

(2009. We thought we were
too big to fail. Wrong again.)

Some year, eh? We all looked for Hope. Then we all looked for Change. Then we all looked for a job. Then, by year's end, we all just hoped that Congress would change jobs.

Let's review.

January
During a bone-chilling outbreak of global warming, Barack Obama was inaugurated President of the United States, and got three votes for the Papacy, and won the Rose Bowl. He immediately set the tone for his administration by having world-class musicians fake a music performance, while not paying their taxes. The new President then introduced us to his "twin-teleprompter" speaking style, making him look like he's constantly talking to 2 very tall voters on opposite sides of the room.

Congress presented a Health Care Bill that everybody agreed was probably well-written.

February
Following an initial review by an independent agency, it was discovered that the Health Care Bill failed to mention doctors, hospitals, disease, medication or Health Care,

though it did exempt "Congressional hubris" as a pre-existing condition. In a spirit of bipartisanship, Congress fired the independent agency and agreed to adjourn until after the 2010 mid-term elections.

A religious group attempted to force its city council to display the "Seven Aphorisms of Summum" next to the Ten Commandments. According to them, these pithy pronouncements were given to Moses along with the more-famous two tablets. The campaign failed, but one of the aphorisms ("Everything Vibrates") was adopted by White House Press Secretary Robert Gibbs to explain the unstable and rapidly-collapsing economy.

Meanwhile, thousands of formerly intelligent corporate executives and financial analysts ran around yelling at each other about "taking a serious haircut" and no, we still have no idea what that means.

March
An enraged McDonald's customer called 911 because the restaurant ran out of McNuggets. President Obama remarked that the deep-fryer personnel had "acted stupidly." Congress responded by appropriating $17 trillion for shovel-ready intestinal caulking projects.

In a calming gesture, Press Secretary Gibbs announced that "Americans should know that we're not talking about raising taxes until the year Two Hundred and Eleven," creating a huge spike in sales of TurboTax (3rd Century Edition). Meanwhile, President Obama counseled that it might be a good time to start investing in the stock market again, citing attractive corporate "profits-to-earnings" ratios.

Profits-to-earnings. Now, we're no financial mavens, but we're guessing that a company's profits-to-earnings ratio would tend to pretty much hover at around 1-to-1. But hey, he's the President.

In a spirit of bipartisanship, Congressional leaders had the locks changed and disconnected their phones.

April
As the Obama honeymoon began to end, some jaded pundits admitted that sometimes they missed Dick Cheney popping in on the Sunday morning news shows and making little teepee shapes with his hands.

The Weather Channel scared everybody to death by announcing that Oklahoma had been hit by "wind-whipped winds." Not to be outdone, New Orleans complained of an onslaught of rain-soaked rain. Congress responded with a non-binding resolution, changing the official name for "weather" to "H1N1."

The multi-thousand-page Health Care Bill fell off a shovel-ready table and landed on the Housing Market, causing the Housing Market to collapse. Press Secretary Gibbs claimed that the table's collapse was inevitable, since "everything vibrates." Meanwhile, General Motors was caught in a video sting, trying to buy young Asian cars from an ACORN employee.

President Obama delivered his one millionth speech and quoted from the Bible, which he apparently borrowed from some Judeo-Christian nation somewhere. In a related story, the owner of a Midwest diner claimed that a stain had miraculously appeared on his griddle that looked a lot like President Obama parting the Delaware River.

May
On Facebook, a "find out what month you were born" quiz was all the rage, prompting the Surgeon General to have Facebook declared a controlled substance. In a related story, Viagra updated its list of side-effects to include "flushing, delayed backache, loss of balance and blurred vision." The Surgeon General pointed out that these may also be the side-effects of sex. Or the Swine Flu. Or Facebook.

President Obama learned how to sign his entire name at one time, thereby saving billions of dollars in redundant ink pen costs during bill signings. Congress immediately spent the savings on shovel-ready solar-powered bike paths for transgendered yogurt addicts.

Due to a clerical error, over 10,000 stimulus checks were sent to dead people. The dead people immediately started their own fan page on Facebook.

In a spirit of bipartisanship, Congress combined the entire nation into a single voting district.

June
President Obama announced that he would complete his second 100 Days in only 72 days, and that on the 73rd day, he would rest.

In California, under tragic and very suspicious circumstances, pop icon Michael Jackson suddenly qualified for a stimulus check.

Millions of young students eagerly wrapped up another school year, after turning in their year-end essays, entitled "How Congress Spent My Summer Vacation."

At a press conference on waterboarding techniques, Nancy Pelosi denied denying her formal denial, explaining that "Well, in that context 'we' did not include me," after which she exited the room through three doors, simultaneously.

July
In its search for creative financing, the Treasury Department took possession of all Monopoly play money. The perennially-popular board game then released a fun "bailout" version, featuring the new "Get Anything Out Of Congress Free" card.

President Obama treated America to a "teachable moment" by way of a Beer Summit, during which Joe Biden leaked the location of SC Governor Mark Sanford. Following the summit, Biden began complaining that "everything vibrates." The Surgeon General declared Joe Biden a controlled substance.

In a spirit of bipartisanship, Congress suspended elections and declared themselves immortal beings.

August
In the stifling late-summer heat, Nancy Pelosi's face finally melted and fell off. In a spirit of bipartisanship, Arlen Specter crossed the aisle and let her borrow one of his.

President Obama won the World Cup soccer tournament, and got an Oscar nomination for "Best Director," and was named Canada's "Woman of the Year."

Due to a clerical error in the Health Care Bill, Congress appropriated $17 trillion for early treatment of "Irritable Vowel Syndrome."

September
The Internet announced it was running out of room, but Al Gore swapped some carbon credits and bought it some more numbers from an ACORN employee. Press Secretary Gibbs reminded us that the White House had inherited math from the previous administration.

Olympic swimming legend Michael Phelps appeared in a compromising photograph, showing him smoking Facebook with Tiger Woods, Paris Hilton, and SC Governor Mark Sanford.

October
Due to an outbreak of the Swine Flu, Halloween was canceled, prompting thousands of new ads offering deals on "scary Christmas costumes." In other marketing news, Rio de Janeiro edged out Chicago for the 2012 Olympic games, citing South America's rich tapestry of arcade-style street violence and Appalachian hiking trails.

President Obama swept the World Series in an unprecedented three straight games. He congratulated himself on his teamwork.

Concerned Colorado residents called 911 after sightings of a giant airborne Jiffy-Pop container. Congress responded by appropriating $17 trillion for shovel-ready "The History of Maize" museums.

In an attempt to boost flagging ticket sales, a commercial airline announced its new "Don't Ask, Don't Tell" shuttle service between Nigeria and Detroit, including a layover along the scenic Appalachian hiking trails of Amsterdam.

November

The Swine Flu was canceled, due to an outbreak of facts.

The world came to the collective conclusion that George W. Bush is the most generous man on Earth, given that everything President Obama owns was apparently inherited from the previous President, including several internal organs.

The Midwest diner's owner with the famous stain complained that the miraculous stain had disappeared, and right in the middle of his Miraculous Stains Of The Midwest Guided Tour And Lunch Buffet, too. Congress responded by appropriating $17 trillion to shovel-ready trans-fat rezoning parity projects.

Senator Ben Nelson made a bunch of new friends when he agreed, in return for selling his Health Care vote, to eternally burden the other 49 states with Nebraska's Medicaid debt. After the bill-signing ceremony, Nelson was given a dictionary, exposing him to lots of evocative new vocabulary words, like "pariah" and "effigy" and "early retirement" and "Faust."

December

A terrorist attack on a commercial airline was narrowly averted, prompting the vacationing President Obama to immediately not cancel his Hawaiian holiday; however,

Press Secretary Gibbs pointed out that the news did force the President to badly shank a drive on the seventh fairway. The media rushed to press with in-depth objective analysis of the First Family's trip to buy Sno-Cones.

According to one news report, passengers noted that the terrorist suspect went to the plane's bathroom, returned and complained that his stomach hurt, and then covered himself with a blanket. Shortly thereafter, passengers heard popping noises and noticed an odor, then realized "the man's leg was on fire," which the Surgeon General warned could also be the side-effects of Viagra. Or the Swine Flu.

And in a spirit of bipartisanship, Congress seceded from the Union.

Head of the Country

(He hit his head. That's it. That's
all that happened. He hit his head.)

Some days ago, the news reported that President Obama had bumped his head on the doorway of Marine One, his official helicopter. And then, as we all watched, the entire planet clutched its collective heart, and lost its collective ever-lovin' mind.

A heartbroken CNN quickly announced a mourning vigil, and API set up a skull bureau. MSNBC threw together a Support Obama's Head Phone Center, and immediately fielded calls from both their remaining viewers. *The New York Times* launched an investigative series into helicopter door budget shortfalls, and another probe into helicopter door cost overruns. Geraldo Rivera posted an exposé on the rising incidence of head bumps in Aruba. Celebrity lawyer Gloria Allred offered her services, in case anybody anywhere wanted to sue anybody for anything. And FoxNews issued a "FoxNews Alert," as they tend to do every 11 seconds or so.

The rogue helicopter was quickly wrestled to the ground by alert White House security and then transported to Gitmo for what would surely be an intense interrogation, including the dreaded and publicly unpopular tactic of "skateboarding." As a security measure, Vice President

Biden was spirited away to an undisclosed location, where he bumped his own head on Dick Cheney, who then mistakenly shot the attending Secret Service agent. Meanwhile, the President was rushed to the hospital to be thoroughly checked out, but no X-rays or MRIs were necessary, due to the President's policy of total transparency.

An independent astronomer in Chicago noted an unusually high psychic activity level among empaths in the Rigel star system, an observation that was confirmed by three Wise Men. Conspiracy theorists were quick to blame the helicopter incident on an insidious vast no-wing conspiracy. Code Pink sympathizers rushed to pink-mob-strength outside the White House fence, waving pink, hand-lettered, misspelled, grammatically-incorrect signs, displaying timely, relevant slogans like "AMERICA IS THE GREAT SANTA," whatever *that* means.

An ad hoc Congressional inquiry sprang up, in which several members pointed out that the helicopter had not been built in their districts, which is really unfair, because they were firmly on record as being solidly pro-helicopter. Further funding was appropriated in order to insure that unemployed helicopter maintenance technicians would not lose their pensions, and a couple of banks, chosen at random, were given 400 billion dollars.

Shortly, White House mouthpiece Robert "Obviously" Gibbs released a comforting public statement, containing several actual verbs. "Obviously, we're looking into this, and though I obviously don't want to get ahead of things, I, you know. Obviously, our administration inherited that helicopter. All the evidence isn't in, obviously, but it clearly looks to be George Bush's fault. We, um." Gibbs firmly denied the rumor that First Lady Michelle Obama, upon hearing the news, had been so distraught that she nearly bought a dress off-the-rack.

A spokesperson for the helicopter refused to comment.

Weak in the News

(Some of this is true. None of it ought to be.)

Last week, every time I watched the news, weird things were happening. Odd, dim, dumb, disjointed events. Bizarre behavior. Confusing commentary. A feast of folly.

Witness:

Monday
In an effort to create jobs, Congress allocated $50,000 to three puppet theaters. The White House applauded the news, claiming that it saved or created seven socks.

In Norway, President Obama accepted the Nobel "Peace Eventually" Prize. The White House applauded the news, claiming that it saved or created 2 Nobel Awards Committee jobs. Obama then read a speech, in which he explained European history to the Europeans. Then he flew off to accept the Nepalese "Yak of the Year" award.

The EPA classified Carbon Dioxide as a pollutant. Joe Biden advised all Americans to "do the patriotic thing" and stop exhaling. All the world's plants and trees collectively filed a grass-action lawsuit. Their spokes-fern cited "photosynthesis bias."

An unnamed scientist released a film showing an octopus sitting in a coconut shell, then dragging the shell somewhere else, then sitting in it again. Excited scientists called this the first evidence of a non-mammal using tools, unless you count film-maker Michael Moore.

President Obama absolutely insisted that Congress pass the Health Care Bill by Christmas.

Tuesday
Faced with an obscene $12 trillion debt, Congress organized a hostile takeover of board-game giant, Parker Brothers, after discovering that the game company had a big pile of available Monopoly money. Congress then invoked a seldom-used parliamentary procedure, the "Cosmically Stupid" rule, allowing them to borrow more money than actually existed in the physical universe.

In an interview with Oprah, President Obama gave himself a B+ grade, apparently oblivious to the fact that he had a public approval rating of negative 8% (negative 16% if you count both teleprompters). Pundits presume he gave himself a B simply because his name starts with a B. President Obama responded by having his name changed to "Arack."

An unnamed scientist released a film showing Al Gore eating octopus in the company of a waitress wearing coconut shells. Citing a seldom-used parliamentary procedure, Al invoked Semi-Executive Privilege and had the scientist boiled down into a carbon credit. The octopus could not be reached for comment, though close friends claim it's having its name changed to "Aractopus."

Fed Chairman Ben "Trust Me" Bernanke and Tiger "Call Me" Woods were both featured on magazine covers, prompting rumors that one or both of them had fathered Brad Pitt's love child. The octopus invited Brad to a luau.

President Obama absolutely insisted that Congress discuss the Health Care Bill by Christmas.

Wednesday
The Transportation Security Administration (TSA) mistakenly posted their secret "airport screening" tactics on the Internet, and al Qaeda responded by inserting an armed virgin into every bag of complimentary peanuts. Not to be outdone, Amtrak issued a clerical error, mandating that all passengers carrying guns on board be locked in a box. Not the guns: the passengers.

In an effort to create jobs, Congress allocated $95,000 to a university to catalog Icelandic pollen. Pollen stocks soared, or would have, if there were any pollen stocks.

President Obama closed Gitmo, prompting the mainstream media to crow that he had fulfilled yet another campaign promise. Fifteen minutes later, Obama reopened Gitmo. Oddly, the mainstream media missed the story.

An Illinois politician proudly announced that the Gitmo detainees would be transferred to an empty prison in Illinois. The White House applauded the news, claiming that it will save or create many new prisoners, not to mention dozens of Arabic license plates. About 2 hours later, all the relocated Gitmo detainees escaped and took the politician hostage. The White House applauded the news, claiming that it saved or created many new law enforcement jobs, not to mention a job opening for an Illinois politician. Bidding for the Illinois office began immediately.

President Obama absolutely insisted that Congress read the Health Care Bill by Christmas.

Thursday
800,000 Swine Flu vaccines were recalled after testing uncovered that they were utterly, totally useless. Despite similar test results, nobody in Congress is recalled. Frustrated parents were given a free lead-laced Chinese toy.

An environmental group in the Pacific Northwest pressed to outlaw tying yellow ribbons to some trees, claiming it to be unfair to other trees. The trees could not be reached for comment, since they had formed an Aractopus Coalition and were busy picketing Al Gore's house.

Harry Reid found several missing billions in Medicare money, and was then spotted walking down a Washington street, randomly shoving quarters into parking meters.

President Obama absolutely insisted that Congress learn how to spell either "health" or "care" by Christmas.

Friday
Al Gore threatened that the earth would collapse into a ball of fire by next weekend, quoting a scientist who told him that all the ice in the Arctic Circle would melt, next Tuesday at noon. The scientist called Al a soulless liar, prompting Al to haughtily respond that he did, too, have a soul, but he misspelled it "sole," prompting the octopus

to construct a coconut-based reconnaissance drone to fly over Al's house, looking for fish.

In a freak winter storm of historic proportions, Washington received over 14 inches of global warming.

President Obama gave up on passing Health Care, but he absolutely insisted that somebody in Congress pass a kidney stone by Christmas.

Saturday
And then, at the end of this staggeringly silly week, something even more odd happened. Like an episode of 'Seinfeld,' everything suddenly fell into place. Suddenly, it all made sense.

Witness:

Gitmo detainees again escaped from the Illinois prison, captured Wrigley Field in 2 innings, renamed a famous Chicago landmark the "Sears Minaret," and were hired as Amtrak security guards by the TSA.

Sick of all the anti-plant slant, disgruntled trees stormed an Amtrak sleeper car, quickly routing a cadre of Gitmo detainees wearing "Cubbies Rule" caps. The trees armed themselves, destroyed a yellow ribbon factory in Chicago, and leveled Al Gore's house.

Congress chopped down a bunch of right-leaning trees and printed more Monopoly money. Wind-borne pollen from the felled timber created a pollen pandemic. China sold us an all-new pollen vaccine, and six dozen more Zhu

Zhu pets. Congress issued a clerical error, mandating that all small children receive a Zhu Zhu pet intravenously.

All the global warming in Washington melted, precipitating a rapid rise in ocean levels. The octopus built an outboard motor constructed of coconut fibers and detritus from Al Gore's house and motored into Georgetown. The octopus crashed a White House dinner, where it was served by a sock puppet who kept trying to show it a screenplay.

After dinner, the octopus was introduced to Tiger Woods in a DC bar. After a few Mai Tai rounds, the octopus fell head-over-tentacles for Tiger, and they conceived a son.

And a young unknown named Aractopus Obama claimed to have cured pollen cancer, and announced his run for the 2012 Presidential race.

Ale to the Chief

(Tastes great? Less filling?)

[Obama] Gentlemen, welcome to the White House Beer Summit, a totally unscripted glorification of my leadership, with just a few hundred randomly-positioned photographers. Thank you both for joining me here today. This promises to be an outstanding example of my massive outreach skills.

[Crowley] Thanks for the invite, sir, but I don't see any beer.

[Gates] Hey, what's with the white table and chairs?

A waiter arrives with the three most famous beers in human history. These beers have been researched, challenged, interviewed, and submitted to a brutal yeast analysis by the Senate. All three beers have received reality show offers. One is in therapy.

As the waiter nears the table, a Secret Service agent leaps from the shrubbery, tasers the waiter, and frisks the beers.

[Obama] Thank you, waiter.

[Waiter] Agghh. Ahk.

[Obama] Oh, and waiter?

[Waiter] Aaaaahhng?

[Obama] Bring me a non-divisive tablecloth.

The agent drags the waiter away and returns with a grey General Motors guest towel.

[Secret Service] Best I could do, sir.

[Obama] How's that, Professor?

[Gates] Appropriate. What's with the extra chair?

[Obama] The ghost of Eleanor Roosevelt has been channeling me, begging me for leadership advice. The empty chair symbolizes my massive outreach skills.

[Crowley] Uh, yeah. Whew. Man, look at the time! Well, thanks for the brewski, Mister Presi…

[Obama] Mr. Crowley, a moment, please. I have several more leadership moments to share. Remember, this is a teachable moment for America. Give me a moment more of your time.

[Crowley] That's a whole lotta moments, sir.

[Obama] Ease up. I'm reciting these lines from memory.

The agent leans in.

[Secret Service] Excuse me, sir, but you have an incoming 'flash' call from codename Harpo, sir.

[Obama] Code which?

[Secret Service] From the Vice President, sir.

[Obama] "Harpo?"

[Secret Service] You know, like Harpo Marx, sir. The guy who never spoke? Just a little agency humor, sir, common among brilliant, under-appreciated security professionals. Sir.

[Crowley] Good one, agent.

[Gates] You know, "Harpo" spelled backwards is "Oprah." What's that supposed to mean?

Obama takes the phone from the agent.

[Obama] Yes, Joe? Going well. Have you finished the jigsaw puzzle, Joe? You sure? Even the sky? You wanna do what? Joe, that's just not a good ide … Joe, it's not an extra chair, it's Eleanor's cha … okay. Okay! Five minutes, then straight to bed, okay? Uh huh … yes … yes, I love you, too, Joe.

Joe Biden runs up and sits down. He's dressed exactly like Obama, but Joe sports an "I'm With The Big Guy" baseball cap.

[Joe] Hello, gentlemen! And you, too, Big Guy!

[Obama] Joe…

[Joe] What'd I say? How goes it, Professor? Officer?

[Crowley] All good, here. You?

[Gates] A pleasure to see you, Mr. Vice President. We were just enjoying a nice ale with your boss.

[Joe] What? No malt liquor? Just kidding, Teach. Hey, Teach, didja hear the one abou …

[Obama] Joe…

[Joe] What?

[Gates] It's okay, Mr. President.

[Joe] Well, this is cozy, eh? White, black, white, black. Maybe we ought to haul in a Supreme Court nominee as a tie-breaker, eh? Ha!

[Obama] Joe…

[Joe] Are those cashews? Man, I love cashews! How 'bout you guys?

[Gates] I certainly enjoy an après-dinner kernel or two, Mr. Vice President, perhaps accompanied by a petite pomme and fine aperitif.

[Joe] A who? Whoa. Hey, Teach, you expectin' change back from that eight-dollar sentence?

[Obama] Joe…

[Joe] No way some stupid cop would gab like that, eh, Big Guy?

[Obama] Joe, that's eno…

[Joe] But cocktail nuts, they really tear me up, if know what I'm sayin'. How 'bout you, Joe Friday? You, too? Hey, wanna see a trick?

[Crowley] Yes, sir?

[Joe] Pull my finger!

[Obama] JOE!

[Joe] Wha-ha-ha-t?

How Congress Spent My Summer Vacation

(Some call it "global warming."
We call it "summer.")

August in America. It's hot. But the simple word "hot" doesn't really do justice to this collision of cruelties, this hellish mix of heat, humidity and no football. It's so hot that the TV weather people - who all have names like Tempe, and Biff, and Bink - start making up "hot" alternate words like "convection" and "dew point" and "the feels like temperature" and "Do tonight's remote from *where?* South Florida? In *August?* Get my agent on the phone!"

August. It's so hot that in downtown Detroit half the buildings are on fire, unlike mid-winter, when downtown Detroit is freezing, and half the buildings are on fire. It's so hot that it melts the vital stupidity inhibitors in people's brains, prompting normally clever people to corner you in public places, grinning broadly and yelling things like "So! Hot enough for ya?"

I've never understood that convivial communication. Hot enough? I'm drenched in sweat and the side of my head that's closest to the equator looks like a Salvador Dali painting. That's just about hot enough for me, yes. Thanks for asking!

Why is heat special? I mean, in the face of other adversities, we're not sadistically teased about it; we're not constantly queried. Nobody ever points to your bee sting, or that swelling you picked up after that dare involving some crazy glue and a squid, grins broadly, and asks, "So! Infected enough for ya?"

"So! Hot enough for ya?" On the Just-Be-Quiet-O-Meter, that's right up there with "So! Working hard, or hardly working?" and "I tell you what!" which, in the South, is a complete sentence.

August. Hot, yes. But life must go on. Congress, just back from their Fourth of July break, took the whole month of August off as a paid vacation, just like you and I get to do every year. But suddenly, House Speaker Salvador Pelosi ordered them all back to Washington to approve some more spending, using some more imaginary money that she'd forgotten to dream up earlier. (This clutch of clowns can't even get a *vacation* right.) But, selfless public servants that they are, they wasted no time and got right down to Minding The People's Business, holding closed-door debates on crucial national security issues, like banning chewing tobacco in Pro Baseball.

Nor was academia sitting around this summer, twiddling their thumbs. Scientists in the theoretical mathematics department at MIT finally came up with a number large enough to accurately measure Glenn Beck's systolic blood pressure. It's hoped that this astronomically massive new uber-integer will finally allow mortal science to calculate the President's ego.

And speaking of the President: in August, after checking poll results, the White House announced that it was the President's birthday. Conservative pundits immediately complained about the President scheduling a critical birthday event during a Congressional recess.

But citizens rushed to flood the White House with birthday greetings, some signed, some sent anonymously, plus one that never got delivered at all, after it was allegedly purchased and then allegedly vanished. (Representative Charlie Rangel insisted it was an "oversight" and he looks forward to a full and open investigation.) Shortly, it was discovered that the majority of the greeting cards were made by Hallmark, causing the American Greetings card company to apply for a federal bailout, which was denied.

(I'm just kidding, obviously, about the American Greetings part. Of *course* they weren't denied a bailout.)

Moreover, we've been able to get a peek at some of the actual birthday cards the President received, thanks to a top-shelf, selfless, public-service-oriented website named "wiki leaks," which may be the dumbest name for a website since "TheFeelsLikeTemperature.com." Let's take a look:

- Happy Birthday! So glad to hear that you DO have a birth certificate!
- Happy Birthday! Should today be a federal holiday, or a religious holiday?
- Happy Birthday! (This large green card was funded by the American Recovery and Reinvestment Act)
- Happy Birthday! Hope you enjoy the nice election we bought you. Love, the AFL-CIO

- Happy Birthday! I miss you so much. Madame Speaker (guess what I'm wearing)
- Happy Birthday! Sorry this card is late - I know that, in Indonesia, it's already tomorrow.
- Happy Birthday! Karl sends his best. Meet me in the graveyard at midnight and I'll give you the plans for phase two. Vladimir
- Happy Birthday, 44! Hillary & I sure did miss you at the wedding!
- Happy [censored] Birthday from the Blagojevich family! Your [censored] present is under the troll in the [censored] Rose [censored] Garden, you [censored] bag of [extremely censored].

But even a summer like this one eventually comes to an end. Summer vacations are wrapping up, and kids are getting ready to go back to school. Many eager youngsters will be required to compose that standard summer's end essay, "How I Spent My Summer Vacation." Not many eager youngsters will actually turn in the project, however, because they're all too bitter about school-banned junk food, or too busy learning how to don school-supplied condoms.

So let's give the kids a hand. Let's share some of the books we've read this summer and get those creative writing juices flowing. For those who waited till the last minute to begin their end-of-summer essay, here's a handy list of some very, very short reads:

- "Hee-Haw's Most Hilarious Episodes"
- "America's Favorite Raw Pork Recipes"

- "How To Keep A Secret" by Joe Biden
- "Award-Winning Segments On MSNBC"
- "Women I Highly Respect" by Bill Clinton
- "A More Effective Muslim Outreach: NASA's Best Ideas"
- "Our Relevant Opinions On Stuff" by Lady Gaga, Jimmy Carter and Prince
- "Great Barbecuing Ideas Using Bifidus Regularis"
- "Gangsta Rap's Contributions to Love Ballads"
- "The Compleat List Of Satisfied Prius Owners"
- "Things That Are My Fault" by Barack Obama

Extra credit essay question: In 250 words or less, list any expressions you can think of that are funnier than "don a condom."

Planet of the Trousered Apes

Area 51 & the Water Witches

(Vegas voodoo, pollo politics,
and one alien's quest for tenure)

Well, thanks to some over-achievers in Reno, Nevada, we're about to lose another Constitutional freedom: our inalienable right to vote while wearing a chicken costume.

According to my exhaustive research (assisted by two data collection experts from British Petroleum running around the Gulf with a tape measure), Nevada state officials have been forced to add chicken costumes to their growing list of items that are banned at public polling places. I can't wait to find out what else is on their "banned at the polls" list. Ferrets, maybe? Voters?

Like many extremely stupid things, it all began innocently. Among the 12 current Republican primary candidates in Nevada is a woman, a nice Republican lady who, like most of us, is a millionaire casino executive and a former beauty queen. As part of her "Look How In Touch I Am With The Little People" political platform, the nice lady recently suggested that people barter with their doctors, just like when her grandparents used to "bring a chicken to the doctor."

Now, if you or I walked in to a doctor's office holding a chicken, it wouldn't go well. We'd probably be referred immediately to a tweed-wearing specialist with a goatee and a name like Altoid von Munchkin. But maybe the nice lady's grandma, back in her pre-golden years, didn't have veterinarians in Nevada. Or maybe all the veterinarians were busy moonlighting in Vegas casinos, half-naked in 10-inch stiletto heels and sequined skullcaps.

The nice Republican lady and her eleven opponents are all competing for the chance to run against Majority Leader Harry "Altoid" Reid, who's been Senator in Nevada since the day his ship crash-landed in nearby Roswell, New Mexico. And I'm guessing that each of the other 11 candidates has their own cute farm animal anecdote to share, too; their own memories of Granny and her haunting medical habits.

But political emotions are running deep in 2010, and when the clever Democrats in Nevada heard about the chicken quip, they responded like sensible, intelligent, reality-grounded career politicos, employing time-tested tenets of rock-solid political theory: they crashed their opponent's campaign events with volunteers wearing chicken suits.

Responding in kind, with a proud dignity reminiscent of classic political discourse in ancient Greek culture, the Republicans bought a bunch of TV time and started whining. As a result, chicken costumes are now banned in Nevada within 100 feet of polling places. Political shirts, hats and signs are also banned, just in case some rogue rooster shows up wearing a partisan Bojangles beanie or waving a "No More Omelets!" placard, and if you've ever visited Vegas, you know this is not entirely outside the realm of possibility.

A local party partisan carped that wearing chicken outfits while exercising one's right to vote would be "inappropriate," effectively transmitting an obvious anti-Nice-Republican-Lady message. A Nice-Republican-Lady spokeshuman said ... and I'm not good enough to make this stuff up ... "I think most voters are going to the polls thinking about far greater things than Harry Reid's chickens."

Most voters? *Most?*

In these odd days, there are hundreds of relevant, vital, life-altering issues on the minds of the voting public. For instance, where do the candidates stand on poultry-based bio-fuel? Are these undocumented hens? Can British Petroleum use chickens to plug that geyser in the Gulf?

I suppose, given their proximity to California, there are bound to be a few tin-foil-hat types that want to hear more about the critical Chicken Angle in this story. Well, fear not. I'm your man. And I'm wearing the boots to do it.

Admittedly, we don't yet know if these are naturalized chickens, or if they were hatched right here in this Best Of All Possible Nations If You Live For Ridiculous News Stories. But make no mistake: immigration is going to a front-burner issue in the 2010 mid-term elections. And it's almost impossible for any reasonable, thinking person to deny the logic underlying one simple syllogism:

1. The United States shares a southern border with Mexico;
2. Immigrants are entering the United States by crossing the southern border with Mexico;

3. So it logically follows that the immigrants are quite likely to be ... what? You got it. Swedish.

Now, I'm not here to muddy up my story by injecting any actual facts. But as it turns out, the chicken has a long and illustrious place in the histories of Sweden and our other southern neighbors. There are thousands of historical documents which, for very good reasons, I haven't shared with you, that validate the importance of the chicken in the rich cultures of Meso-America. (literal translation: "Before the Spanish showed up, this place rocked")

You should know that in some parts of Mexico, and downtown Sweden, chicken is called "pollo." (pronounced "yard bird") Other countries do that a lot - it's almost seems, sometimes, that they have a different word for just about everything. Pretty rude, when you think about it. I mean, if English was good enough for the Old Testament, it ought to be good enough for Sweden and its next-door neighbor, Peru.

Marketing Sidebar: Due to extremely negative focus group feedback, "Kentucky Fried Pollo" never really caught on in Nevada. On the other hand, Swedish caterers don't care much for Peruvian Meatballs.

As we all know, Mexico is the home of the famous pyramid-slash-temple named Chichen Itza. (literal translation: "Jaguar? Tastes like chicken.") Within these time-worn walls, ancient mystics and millionaire casino executives would gather together to play an ancient form of basketball, and then round out the afternoon by throwing people into a well. This spectator-participation sport dates back to an even more ancient, but equally fun, group nicknamed the "Witches of Water," the dreaded "Brujas del Agua." (pronounced "British Petroleum") Then late one afternoon, around three-ish, the Spaniards showed up, having sailed across the Atlantic from Spania, and things got much more civilized. Not really.

Back in Nevada, however, they've a real problem on their hands. Committed partisan voters in chicken costumes are running around the desert with a tape measure, and then congregating exactly 101 feet from polling places. And at this point, I have to wonder - where do you *buy* a chicken costume, much less hundreds of them? And what's the other side wearing? Furry little Coyote Republican hats? Furiously partisan Chicken Hawk costumes?

And the ultimate poser for the political pundits: Why did the chicken cross the aisle?

Aliens for the Twins

*(Fame. Crime. Greed. Gravy
biscuits. What's a girl to do?)*

Here in my town of Creyer (pronounced "Cur"), it's been a right weird week. I mean, between the crime wave, and the City Hall controversy, and the alien auditions, and what-all, people didn't know whether to buck or go sit.

First off, a movie company from out in Hollywood announced it was gonna make a science fiction picture, and film it right here in our state. According to Creyer's weekly paper, the *Literable Gazette*, casting agents would be coming to town, looking to cast extras for the movie.

We're hearing that the movie's to be titled "Ipod" or "Iso-pod." Some such. Maybe it was "Isobar." Anyway, it's supposed to have background alien extras running round all over it, making little background alien extra noises, shooting ray guns, wearing background alien extra tin foil uniforms ... whatever it is that union-scale actors do in-between car chases and catered meals. (By the way, Tyrell, over at Tyrell's Pole Dancing And Lunch Buffet, is angling *hard* for *that* catering plum.)

The director of this new picture is the same fellow that directed that movie "Rain Man" (or as it's known around here, "Forrest Gump: The Prequel").

Best as we could ever make out, "Rain Man" was a movie about some fellow who could count matches real fast. And as I recall, start to finish, not a gun fight nor a car chase to be found. Not one.

This new picture must be a sequel to "Rain Man." That would explain "Isobar." Though I admit it's a stretch, even for a Hollywood director who makes movies about matches.

Bless his heart.

The paper said that all interested folks should show up at the auditions, and bring a photograph of themselves that they won't get back, which, if you ask me, is not a very promising way to start a business relationship. Auditions would be held Wednesday evening at Cotton Mather Elementary School. And that, of course, was the first problem.

Movie auditions on a school night! More worse, the Music Director down at Our Ladies Of Perpetual Gastritis complained that the movie auditions ran up against the Ladies' weekly choir practice. Creyer's Mayor, Carl "Big Carl" Sweeney, had to drive over and try to un-rile up the Ladies.

And that's when the news of the Creyer crime spree broke out.

Now, understand. See, Big Carl hadn't had a great deal of experience with Hollywood, and he reckoned Creyer was facing a virtual invasion of tans and poodles and drugs and breasts. So, he addressed the problem like every other elected official addresses every other problem.

He threw money at it.

Big Carl convinced the city to buy a brace of those "smart" traffic signs, those things that sit on the side of the road and tell you how fast you're going, in case you somehow managed to buy a car that doesn't have a dashboard.

Creyer picked up the pair of smart signs for the rock-bottom-act-now-today-only sale price of only $31,000, which was easily justifiable since Creyer had just received $1.3 million, earlier in the year, for their cooperation in a 2008 Federal video poker sting.

And in this respect, Creyer's politicians are no better nor worse than anybody else's politicians. Free money creates amnesia. Happens all the time. We never learn. Creyer failed to fully grasp the concept that the only reason the federal government has money to give to Creyer in the first place is because, at some point, Creyer sent the federal government the money. Creyer forgot: *it was their money in the first place.* So they bought the smart signs.

But within three days, somebody stole the smart right off the sign.

According to the *Literable Gazette*:

An electronic "smart" traffic sign the Creyer Police Department had set up at Incisor Gap Road off Possum Spleen Road was found bent and twisted with the speed sign missing, authorities said.

Officer Scott "Scooter" Downe, who first visited the crime scene, noted that the trailer's rear legs were bent under, the sign's digital display element was missing and the sign below

it ("*IN A HURRY, ARE YE?*") was bent at the screws where someone tried to remove it by force.

*Additionally, Officer Downe noticed there were drag marks in
the grass where someone had apparently tried to drag off the
whole sign.*

Concerning possible leads or arrests, there was no official
statement from the Creyer Police. But later, we did get an
insightful earful when we ran into Officer Downe, who was
getting pretty liquored up down at Tyrell's. Scooter mum-
bled something about Tommy "Towhead" Grimes, who runs
"Grimes of Passion," that little novelty boutique out by the
landfill. A valid culprit, for sure. No question that Towhead's
always a worthy candidate for a full body cavity search. But I
personally was leaning towards Tookey Ankle, night manager
at Pawpaw's Fine Jewelry And Bait Shop, reckoning he stole
the smart sign so he could clock deer from his tree stand.

During our "possible perp" discussion, Scooter seemed
conflicted, but by that point in his evening, he also seemed
to be deaf, invincible, and trapped in the middle of an
extended vowel movement.

Bless his heart.

All Big Carl knew was that there was still one smart sign left.
He put the city's finest on Super-Double-Special Security
Alert Red. He saw the signals, he smelt the dangers. He knew
Creyer. *If this ain't about to become a full-blown, historicalized
crime wave,* he thought, *well, then, I don't know much.*

Meanwhile, Hollywood fever continued to bubble up in
Creyer. Of course, the young folks got bit the worst; impres-

sionable minds, downright smitten with fantasies of fame and fortune; and the duly smit included Big Carl's twin girls, Euphoria and Carl's Junior. The twins had their sights set firmly on becoming alien extras.

Problem is, the twins are - well - let's say "buffet-enabled." They're right healthy. Euphoria's the only person to ever drive by herself through Atlanta and be given a waiver for the carpool lane. And Carl's Junior, though she has a sweet singing voice, can bring an all-you-can-eat pizza lunch joint to the brink of Chapter 11. When the Burger Prince first put in two drive-thru windows, the girl would place an order at the first window, just to hold her over till the second window. Let's face it: Carl's Junior has a better chance of being cast to play the aliens' mother ship.

Bless her heart.

But Big Carl loves his daughters, and so he thought of a way he might help them achieve their dreams.

Now those of you without sin may cast the first stone. Big Carl's not the first politician to let his judgment get all clouded up over a woman, much less two blood-kin women, much less two blood-kin women who are, cumulatively, about seven pounds away from getting their own Zip Code.

Turns out that the folks in the State Capitol were on another anti-obesity kick, and qualifying city employees could be reimbursed, by the State, up to $24,000 for something called a gastric bypass (there's that "free money" dance again).

Now Big Carl didn't really know what a gastric bypass was, other than it sounded like something that, when it kicked in, he truly wanted to be upwind of it. But he knew that, generally, it involved weight loss. And he knew that his beloved daughters were desperate to get themselves some weight loss, at least until they got the memo that weight loss would involve eating less food.

And with all this upcoming Hollywood uproar, Big Carl definitely knew he could figure out a way to pad the Creyer city payroll by two.

So Big Carl succumbed.

By the time the film crews began to arrive, Big Carl was under indictment, the twins were over-medicated, and the smart sign was still AWOL.

Meanwhile, in a private hunting plat just out by the landfill...

Scooter: *Pull!*

[BAM!]

Tookey: Nice hang time, Scooter!

Scooter: What's the smart sign said?

Tookey: Thirty-two miles an hour.

Towhead: That's partly due to the modifications.

Tookey: What modifications?

Towhead: Hot sauce.

Scooter: Any cats left?

Towhead: 'Bout six.

Scooter: Lock 'n load!

Bless their hearts.

Ozzy and Harriet

(The last reality show, on the
last surviving TV network)

Project: New family comedy. Pilot episode. Target buyer, GBS (Government Broadcasting Service).

Working Title: Ozzy and Harriet

Legal: Pilot episode script approved by all currently-seated Fairness Doctrine Censors. Content scrubbed by the Cotton Mather Internet Police, and FCC Diversity scans confirm it to be non-ecumenical. Submitted project duly notarized by Attorney Admiral Eric Holder, though he hasn't read it yet.

Treatment / Plot Synopsis:

The year is 2020. The Euro-Wars have ended indecisively, due to the onset of a new ice age, which was blamed on Global Warming. In the former European continent, now known as East Bethesda, such commerce as still exists is conducted using the new common currency, Tulips.

Earth's petroleum resources have been entirely depleted, but the Middle East continues to manipulate world economies, as Iran has discovered vast underground pools of indigenous, untapped wind. The United Nations continues to threaten Iran with harsh and crippling sanctions, going to ever-escalating extremes, like cutting off their access to reruns of *Seinfeld*. Somehow, Iran still manages to scoff at these draconian diplomatic measures.

Meanwhile, in North America, the economy is beginning to turn around. Unemployment has dropped to 48%, except in the Mexican-held Tzotzil Territories (formerly California), which boast a booming tourism industry, driven by hotels staffed entirely by illegal American immigrants. In an attempt to divert attention from the oil spill that ultimately swallowed Florida, British Petroleum has coal-bombed Alaska, and the entire state of Hawaii has collectively passed out in a sensimilla-induced stupor.

As a result of a radical Manifest Destiny reinterpretation by the Supreme Court, all other states in the "Lower Forty-Seven" have been annexed by Washington, DC, and are now effectively one massive, federal bedroom community, fondly referred to as Bethesda West. This action also removed the need for all that fussy political "re-districting," which is no longer necessary since the formation of the big-tent Inderepublicrat Tea Party.

Fast food has been outlawed, and all caloric consumption is now regulated by the government. School cafeterias are staffed by scary, snood-sporting ex-East-European gymnasts, just like they've always done. All social services and entitlement programs are now managed by the monolithic Department of Health Welfare, Education Welfare & Just Plain Ole Welfare. The new, cabinet-level Bureau of ACORN is canvassing Chicago cemeteries, touting their "It's Never Too Late" voter outreach initiative, and the Presi-

dent's automated weekly phone message has been modi-
fied to include the tag line, "To hear this message in English, press two."

Pilot Episode:

This hilarious new fun-for-all-ages sitcom follows a quasi-
typical American family that, due to having received a gov-
ernment-managed public education, spells "quasi" with a
"K." Ozzy, the emasculated husband and alleged father, has
discovered to his delight that he can collect unemployment insurance for 99 weeks, which is longer than most
current "shovel-ready" jobs even last. Harriet, a graduate
of Wellesley College with a degree in Aberrant Ferret Psy-
chology (which is redundant), is struggling with issues
about pregnancy being a violation of her inalienable Constitutional rights and is, as a rule, medicated beyond belief.
Their twins, Jody and Buffy, are typical: teen-aged, techno-
savvy, wonderfully-appreciative, doting little bundles of
joy, with hormones raging like a red-lining nuclear reactor.

And like every other household in the new America, the
family is served (and monitored) by Mr/s French, a government-issued mechanical helper-droid. Mr/s French is
a standard Citizen Compliance model, complete with sar-
casm detectors and rotatable genders. In accordance with
the 33rd Amendment (the "political correctness" one), Mr/s
French is not engagingly obese, nor engagingly British, nor
dressed, in an engagingly demeaning way, as a butler.

As our pilot episode begins, we find Harriet in her home
office, where she supports her family by buying and selling
politicians on eBay:

"Harriet!"

"Hoo?"

"Honey, are we out of milk?"

"Yes, Ozzy, but we're out of carb credits until next week. Call Mrs. Kravitz next door and see if she'll swap some."

"No can do. Remember, Mrs. Kravitz had to attend Alternative Religion Sensitivity training, down at the Internal Department of Motor Vehicle Revenue."

"Oh, yeah. How about Barney and Betty, across the street?"

"Isn't this their weekend for mandatory volunteering?"

"Don't trouble yourself, dear. I'll activate Mr/s French and send her over."

"Thanks, Sweets. Don't forget, it's Thursday."

"You're right! Today, Mr/s French is gay."

"Mom!"

"Stop shouting, Buffy."

"But Jody's hogging the surfing-the-internet-naked camera!"

"Jody, share with your sister."

"Aw, c'mon, Mom! I've met a new avatar!"

"Jody, I better not finding out you're tweetbooking that Scout Master again!"

"Typical."

"What's that, dear?"

"The Education Czar says that you and Dad are trapped in your own atavistic paradigm."

"It's an inherent element of our generational zeitgeist, dear."

"Whatever."

"Madam?"

"Yes, Mr/s French?"

"You rang?"

"Oh, yeah, I did. Run over to the Rubbles' and negotiate a couple of carb credits, would you?"

"Madam, I believe the Rubbles are at the Post Office just now, for their weekly Body Mass Index monitoring. But I'll check."

"Love the outfit."

"And I, yours, Madam."

"Buffy, have you sent in your daily Citizen Suggestion on how to stop the oil spill yet?"

"Mo-therrrrr."

Trivial News, Hirsute Pursuits

(How to present all the news when there isn't any)

Thanks to 24-hour television news, we are always up-to-date on world events. But to provide 24 hours of content, somebody somewhere has to be talking to somebody about something, every second of every day.

And sometimes this results in elevating the most useless drivel imaginable to the level of "breaking news." When you hear a TV news hair helmet perkily announce, "Coming up next! Cat obesity is on the rise," you can be pretty sure that Earth is not facing imminent destruction by a rogue asteroid.

At least, not during the commercial break.

This past week was a good example. We learned that the US Department of Justice plans to sue the US CIA for the crime of protecting US citizens from terrorist attacks for eight straight years. And since this is, effectively, a case of our own government suing our own government, we get to pay for both legal teams. Oh, good.

In part, the Justice Department is offended over interrogation techniques, employed by the CIA to extract information from captured terrorist Khalid Sheikh Mohammed (KSM). For some reason, it came as a big surprise to the

DOJ that unhinged religious fanatics wouldn't fall to their knees, weeping uncontrollably, even though we swatted their forearms with the flat edge of a kindergarten ruler.

We all know KSM from his mug shot, an attractive piece of candid photography that makes Nick Nolte's arrest photo look like an air-brushed Brad Pitt. Coincidentally, KSM also holds the league record for body hair. The guy looks like he's smuggling centipedes.

But after some quality time with the CIA, the follicle-rich fiend sang like Ethel Merman on a dessert binge. He confessed to several heinous crimes, including lip-syncing during the Karaoke In Kabul semi-finals, and bringing back Classic Coke. But it's not important that America is safe: what matters is the hurt feelings of the bad guys. It's even been whispered that some CIA sociopath blew second-hand smoke in KSM's face. My heavens. They're just out of control.

Meanwhile, on every channel, a famous Senator passed on, and was buried later that same week.

This just in: a famous singer died in June and still hasn't been laid to rest. No, not Ethel Merman.

And in case you needed any more proof that it was a slow news week, gay penguins reappeared in the news. Let's move on.

On ABC (the All Barack Channel), several hundred thousand reporters staked out the president's family vacation, in case he spoke, or breathed, or sat down, or stood up, or stared thoughtfully. And thanks to some crackerjack investigative reporting, we now know that Obama went to the store.

This just in: one of his daughters bought some gum.

Immediately, online bloggers hunkered down to divine the darker truths: What kind of gum? What brand? Was it regular gum or sugar-free? Did the youngster swallow the gum or spit it out?

This just in: the daughter enjoyed a half-stick of sugar-free gum, manufactured by union workers, without petroleum-based machinery, in a bailed-out eco-friendly American factory. She gave the other half to her father, who had a Secret Service agent chew it for him. The agent, an ex-CIA operative, water-boarded the gum.

President Obama called for a national day of eschewing chewing. The National Rubber Association (NRA), our most vocal gum lobby, protested the pronouncement. Homeland Security raised their color alert to Mint. Al Gore, who invented gum, could not be reached for comment.

In a show of solidarity, Congressional Democrats gathered en masse on the Capitol steps and collectively chewed gum. However, several distinguished members suffered severe injuries when they tried to walk at the same time.

This just in: Bill Clinton was caught attempting to interrogate the Double-Mint Twins.

Film at eleven.

Big Al Busts A Move

(As usual, it's the quiet ones you have to watch.)

The path of history often pivots on the most unlikely events. Unexpected, unusual, unlikely events, like the day an Apple fell on Isaac Newton's head, prompting him to switch to Windows.

Unexpected event: an Austrian Archduke is assassinated. Result? World War I.

Unusual event: a French medical student takes a second look at some bread mold. Result? Penicillin was discovered, causing France to surrender to Walgreens.

Unlikely event: a World Cup referee makes a correct call. Actually, this hasn't happened yet.

But history is a veritable swamp of such seemingly random events, like Obama's choice for Vice President. And as a result, history bends in a slightly new direction. Take, for example, the Presidential election of 2000, which Al Gore lost. Twice. Result? Ultimately, it caused the mild, unassuming civil servant to morph into a Sex Vampire.

Picture it. The day is 8 November 2000, the place, a hotel room in Palm Beach, Florida. The election results are in. George Bush is the new President, a victory based on absolutely nothing at all, other than the irritating, flimsy fact that he received the most votes. Twice.

And then it happened. One of those pivotal moments in history, like the day when Strom Thurmond and Helen Thomas drove Isaac Newton to the hospital and sideswiped the Tower of Pisa. An unlikely cause, an unexpected effect. Let's listen in:

"Darn. Darn, darn, darn."

"Al? You okay?"

"Tipper, I was robbed."

"I know, Al."

"I should have been President."

"Careful, Al. You'll bend your hair."

"It is not fair. It is not fair!"

"Al, remember to practice your contractions."

"I'm am trying to practice them, but it doesn't not come easy."

"Better. Better."

"*It's is not fair!*"

"Well, Al, you *were* Vice-President."

"That *was* fun."

"And you *did* invent the Internet. That worked out well, except for the porn."

"*What?* There's is porn on my Internet?"

"Easy, Al. I'm just teasing you."

"That was certainly a humorous thing to say, Tipper."

"Oh, Al, you almost smiled! C'mere. Let mommy oil your neck bolts."

"It is still not fair. Some legacy. Former Vice-President."

"Well, maybe President is out, but look at the bright side. There's always vice. Ba-da-boom!"

"Hmmm."

"Al! I almost told a joke!"

"Vice. Hmmm."

And history bent.

So here we are, a decade later, and a West Coast masseuse has accused The Mad Prophet Of Ecology of engaging in the kind of unseemly activities usually associated with medieval savages, marauding hordes and members of Congress. Gangsta Al has been charged with "Sexual Abuse III," which was way better than "Sexual Abuse" but not nearly as funny as "Sexual Abuse, The Sequel."

Now, admit it, people. Nobody in this room ever, *ever* thought they would hear the words "Al Gore" and "crazed sex poodle" in the same sentence. After all, this is a man whose broad range of emotive facial expressions range from "Dead Serious" to "Recently Deceased." It's widely known that the FBI uses the ex-Veep's vital signs when they need to recalibrate a baseline for their polygraph machines.

To be sure, the masseuse's "Attack of the Oregon Lust Monster" accusation is still just an accusation. This is still an alleged Humpty Dance claim, still a case of "He Droned, She Said." The Tennessee Wild Thang still deserves his day in court, where he will swear to tell the inconvenient truth, the whole inconvenient truth, and nothing but the inconvenient truth. If an American court can still scare up a Bible.

But according to several credible news reports that I just made up, Captain Babe Magnet appears to be caught up in a deviant downward spiral. Witness:

[a phone rings]

"Tammy's Tanning Salon. Can I help you?"

"*May. May* I help you."

"Oy. Must be a full moon. Okay, chief. MAY I help you?"

"I would like to inquire about a massage."

"I'm sorry, sir. Due to the new Universal Health Care tanning tax, we had to let our masseuse go."

"That is an inconvenient happenstance."

"Whatever, Professor."

"I am told that 75% of tanning salons are owned by females."

"Dude, if you think I'm gonna sit here while y..."

"Are you, personally, at least 75% female?"

"Drop dead in the street, weirdopotamus."

"It is okay. You may trust me. I invented the Internet."

Independent sources have confirmed sightings of Al The Gal-Pal setting up unlicensed "Cash for Kisses" kiosks at carnivals and county fairs across America. Carney operators are understandably upset because, rather than charging for a kiss, Boudoir Boy is actually paying the customers, handing out money from something he calls a "lockbox."

[a phone rings]

"Rod Blagojevich. Talk to me."

"I understand that you have spent over $400,000 on clothing."

"What of it?"

"I further note that you have quite a head of hair."

"Who the..."

"Are you, personally, at least 75% female?"

[understandably censored response]

"It is okay. I won a Nobel Peace Prize."

"Vinnie! Call the Fat Man. We're going for a boat ride."

A week earlier, things took an ugly turn at a fast food franchise when Mr. Mobile Warming misinterpreted the nature of the products being sold at a Las Vegas Chick-fil-A. Witnesses recall a soft-spoken, expressionless man with perfect posture, repeatedly muttering about "Chick-n-Strips." Finally, the strange man left after asking for directions to Wendy's.

[a phone rings]

"White House. Can I help you?"

"Could I speak to Fannie Mae?"

"Al, Fannie Mae is a government program."

"I am sorry to trouble you."

"Remember to practice your contractions."

"I'll will."

"Better. Better."

Handling Pan

(A man, a goat, a shark, and a Lama)

Based on recent news, I guess it's time to update the old expression: behind every good man, there is a good-sized bunch of women.

Everybody in the world knows Tiger Woods. And everybody in the world knows that he's married. Everybody, it seems, except Tiger Woods.

According to one of those reliable news sources that keep us entertained at the grocery checkout with headlines like "Oprah Begins New Diet After Eating Radioactive Alien Baby Born to Brad & Angelina," famous pro golfer Tiger Woods has been spending a bit too much time in the rough; lingering over-long in the long grass. While playing the golf course of his connubial commitments, Tiger cheated on his scorecard.

His wife finally caught on, due to Tiger's clever ploy of reading emails from a mistress while his wife was standing right behind him. Then, according to sources, she presented her ruling, got teed off, and teed up upside his head.

Hours later, after she had killed his car, Tiger's handlers spirited him away, announcing to the press that he was a victim of Sax Addiction. Tiger then checked in for a few weeks of Twelve-Side-Steps therapy at the exclusive Palm Springs rehab center, "Kutton Corners," where he underwent a brutal detoxification regimen that required him to surrender all his Marvin Gaye CDs.

Of course, somebody soon unearthed the mistress, who described herself as "a victim" and "like, totally devastated and stuff" and "currently entertaining movie offers." The poor victim, it turns out, was a bit of a celebrity herself, having starred in a whole series of movies, the kind of movies that rarely bother with a sustained plot, and almost never include any television evangelists.

As this news broke, Victim Radar Alerts went off at the compound of celebrity attorney Gloria "Vlad" Allred, the biggest land shark of all time. Mme. Allred, whose business card budget exceeds the GDP of several European nations, leapt off the back of an ambulance and spot-welded herself to the ex-film queen. She dragged the poor victim on TV to cry in public, and furiously began looking for accusatory angles so she could get busy suing people.

It didn't take long. Apparently, at some point during their affair, the film star fell in love with Tiger, after he shared with her those magical words that every love-struck woman wants to hear: "There's no other woman in my life but you, and my wife." And then he broke her heart.

No. Who saw *that* coming?

Now, to be fair to Tiger, I saw a film clip of the jilted woman, standing in profile, just after Ambulance Allred's tort-a-thon. And as a lover of art, I bow in respect. I always like to hunt for that just-right word, and in this situation, that word is "Wow." I have no doubt that Tiger loved her ... for a minute. She was something. When the jiltee stood up and swung sideways, she knocked over a ficus in the next room. I mean, the woman is Thelma AND Louise.

And this week, Tiger showed up in a well-orchestrated, tightly-scripted, televised apology, which certainly had its memorable moments, like when Tiger stared into the camera and said, "I just want to say that [pause-mississippi-1, pause-mississippi-2, pause-mississippi-3] I'm sorry."

The speech had some subliminal elements, too: "I am very sorry [Nike], but you [Gillette] should know that I am now totally [Titleist] focused on my [Wheaties] recovery and my [Trojan] family's recovery."

And then there were some somber insights:

"I accept that I am one of the three most well-known humans on this planet, but I must insist that the press just ignore this whole story."

"No, my wife has never, ever attacked me or any of my fleet of cars. And no, those are not tire tread marks. It's a, uh, a tattoo."

Lastly, Tiger thanked his mom and then informed the world, on national television, that he is a flutist.

And then it all made sense. Flutist! He's come face-to-face with his Sax addiction. Tiger admits that he's a pupil of Pan, that famous, flute-playing half-man, half-goat ... history's most infamous, carefree, party half-animal. The saxophone was simply his gateway drug, inexorably leading to the flute! And the first step to recovery is admitting you have a problem! Obviously, they're making some very positive progress down there at Kutton Corners.

Even the Dalai Lama popped up to offer some redemptive advice, mostly revolving around the role of self-discipline, and the importance of keeping your trailing arm straight when using a long iron. The holy man then took the opportunity to announce his brand-new album, "Yak Kitty Sax," featuring that one-note favorite, "Taking Om Chants On Love."

But the bitter ex-mistress, we now know, was just Victim Number One. Tiger's been caught in so many personal indiscretions that he's now become eligible to run for public office in South Carolina.

I know, I know. Technically, this would qualify his candidacy in just about any other state, too. But it's not the same. Those other states are just pikers. South Carolina is in a league of its own. Remember, we have a Governor who confuses carnal knowledge with camping out; who thinks Argentina is part of the Appalachian trail.

Still not convinced? We've also got a guy in South Carolina, a private citizen, who was charged with Biblically knowing a horse.

Twice.

And it was the same horse.

No matter. With this target-rich bimbo eruption, Tiger is bound to get sued. According to sources, his wife is putting together a revised pre-nuptial agreement that'll dwarf Gloria Allred's business card budget. But who knows? Maybe he can cop a plea:

Judge: Mr. Woods, you stand accused. How do you plead?

Tiger: Mulligan, your honor.

So let's all wish the man well. Let's hope he can kick the flute monkey, stay off the sax, and put Pan behind him. After all, we don't know what demons he's dealing with. Personally, I've never seen a half-man, half-goat.

But someday, I *would* like to see that horse.

Razing Arizona

(Pets. Politics. Aztecs. Angst.
Just another week in America.)

I heard on the news that there may be as many as 20 million pets in the United States, many of them here illegally. You have to admit that this is getting out of control.

Now, before you start firing off a heated response, let's be clear. Nobody is anti-animal. In America, all pets are welcome. Well, maybe not those monster Burmese Pythons in Florida. They've over-populated so much that they've been spotted voting in Palm Beach. And maybe not pet spiders. And ferrets, as a dinner table guest, I can do without. But you get my point. We welcome pets. We always have. And unlike some other countries, we almost never eat them.

Earlier this week, traffic in Tucson ground to a halt as thousands of protestors held rallies and staged marches to protest Arizona's new border-management initiative, nicknamed Don't Bark, Don't Tell. Now, to be fair to the Grand Canyon State, Arizona *has* borne the brunt of a massive influx of pets, like Chihuahuas, illegally crossing the Mexican border in search of a better life, or to avoid being eaten.

And it's not just Chihuahuas. There have been numerous sightings of gangs of tattooed coyotes and tiny Mexican Hairless, loping across the border, donning gang colors, and making crude, untoward remarks to hapless coed border collies.

According to my research, performed in-between updates from Florida's Governor about which political party he was in this week, the Mexican Hairless has been around for over 3,000 years, like the Coffee-Mate in my fridge, and Dick Clark. And never once in all that time did the breed's agent contact a marketing department to brainstorm for a better name than "Mexican Hairless."

The official name for the Mexican Hairless is Xoloitzcuintle (pronounced "Show-low-its-queen-tli"), though it's also known as the Tepeizeuintli (pronounced "Oh, stop it. You're just making that up"). I have no idea what a queen's "tli" is, but I promise to research that, too, just as soon as Florida's Governor switches political affiliations again. Unless he simply gives up and marries Arlen Specter.

But I can share with you this nugget of knowledge from my research about the Xolo, and this is an exact quote: "The hairless Xolo should never be hairy."

Whew. You gotta admire pure, hard science.

According to that same think tank, you should never treat the Xolo like a human, else it may suffer from Small Dog Syndrome. Okay, look. Here's an extremely diminutive quadruped, with a tail, no hair, and ears like a bat, that destroys furniture, often runs around in circles, and, occasionally, shuts up. Personally, I'm not likely to confuse that creature with a human. Congressman, maybe. Human? Nah.

Long, long ago, the Xolo were considered sacred by the Aztecs, except when the Aztecs were eating them. So I guess we can't really blame them when they make a run for the border. In America, at least, they may be able to get a job that American pets don't want, like wearing silly knitted sweaters, or goose-stepping about at American Kennel Club events. Hollywood starlets might drape them in diamonds and carry them everywhere. They might even aspire to participate in the Kentucky Derby, the oldest continuous sporting event in the United States, if you don't count Manifest Destiny.

Meanwhile, Arizona is up to its cactus in politically-polarizing pets; mired in this quadruped quandary. Irate citizens across the country are angry at Arizona, and not just because Arizonans mispronounce "Gila monster." Remember, Arizona also has days in December that can reach 428 thousand degrees Centigrade, and locals will still look you straight in the eye and say, "Yeah, but it's a *dry* heat."

It's heating up politically, as well. Anti-Arizona boycotts are being threatened. And if I know political correctness, get ready for girlcotts, too.

Welcome to Severed Oaths!

(Helpful tips on getting other people to help you
with self-help)

Thanks for your recent registration to the Severed Oaths Self-Help Workshop. We're pleased to let you know that we have accepted your application, based on the following stringent analysis:

1. Your psychological profile is a near-perfect match for our self-help program
2. Your "Why My Life Is A Cold, Bitter, Dark Hole" essay touched our hearts
3. Your check cleared

So to help you prepare for our immersive, world-class experience, we've enclosed a little background information, and some anti-nausea medication. See you soon!

What is Severed Oaths?

Severed Oaths is not a place ... it is a concept, an idea, a non-entity; in other words, a tax-exempt corporate money laundry. And as a "laundry," we're here to cleanse the pocketbook as well as the spirit.

A leader in the management of internal self-loathing since, oh, a really long time ago, Severed Oaths has culled and coerced the best and the brightest from various arenas of personal, political, social and anti-social climates to bring you a diverse and altogether new climate of neuroses.

We focus on things that have been ignored. We look reality in the face. We believe in taking life by the horns, then ripping off one of the horns and, using the horn, beating life to death.

We don't do sacred cows. We insult stuff. We run roughshod over tradition; we ride herd on religious fallacies; we have our own brand. And we could go on for days exploiting this "bull" metaphor. Believe me.

Severed Oaths - a tradition of trust, a playground of the cosmos, a tax deduction. Let's begin!

SEVERED OATHS: PROGRAM HIGHLIGHTS

A Dianetic Approach to World Ecology

Our fragile planet's delicate ecosystems are collapsing, hourly, due to global warming, de-forestation, ozone depletion and environmental exploitation. Species are vanishing as fast as our breathable air supply.

WE. DON'T. CARE.

Our jaded counselors and free-style taxidermists will refocus your priorities in an intensive and patented "Bronx Cheer" approach to the ridiculous whimperings of environmentalists. Day 1 promises to skewer convention by means of our highly popular "Pin the Tail on the Egret" contest. And in another Severed Oaths first, former Reagan-era

Secretary of the Interior James "Buster Quota" Watts will deliver the motivational opening address, entitled "Guns Don't Kill Animals. You Need Bullets, Too."

Award ceremonies and endocrine baths will be held at our exclusive shore-side retreat, "Club Baby Seal." Drinks, lures, ammo, nets and falsified hunting licenses will be provided.

Program Leaders: Alice Cooper & Janet Reno

Sponsor: Pier One Imports

The Art Of The War Of Business

Severed Oaths is proud to offer its new program for upper-echelon corporate management training. In this intensive series of power breakfasts, we ready fledgling power brokers for an active and productive lifetime of ignoring public outcry and denouncing obvious truths. Our hardly qualified phalanx of speakers will address these, among other timely topics:

- Valium: It's Not Just For Breakfast Anymore
- Hostile Makeovers: The Changing Role of the Woman Executive
- The Paperwork Explosion, or "Khrushchev's Last Laugh"
- Corporate Responsibility, Hansel & Gretel, Ulysses and Other Myths
- A Jug Of Wine, A Loaf Of Bread And Thou: A New Approach To Corporate Advancement

Program Leaders: Tim Geithner & Michael Milken

The Holistic Way to Self-Regulation

The path to self-actualization, cosmic harmony and intestinal regularity is a goal we all should seek, some more than others. In this course, we will attempt to achieve these goals through meditation and applied bran ingestion. We will discuss various scatological arguments, such as why those Geico Cavemen always wear that urgent, nervous expression. In our search for the ultimate deity-agnostic diuretic, we will consider various scripts from network sitcoms, hours of C-SPAN footage and the collected culinary works of Chef Boyardee.

Program Leaders: Mel Brooks & Bart Simpson

Sponsor: Taco Bell

Consciousness Expansion/Emotional Release: A Three-Week Search for Mother Nature

As Marshall McLuhan aptly noted, the world has become a "vast wasteland," thanks to the proliferation of television, non-returnable plastics and people who type stuff like "ROTFL!!!" and "Their going, an we r going 2! LOL!" Based on time-proven sales techniques, our staff will lead the intrepid subscribers of this course on an extensive, seven-state tour of the South, offering each day the possibility of venting one's pent-up wrath on completely innocent American homeowners.

Armed only with a broken vacuum-cleaner and a regiment of drunken, syphilitic Union soldiers, participants in this radical program will be forced to confront their darkest psychic arenas as they attempt to sell worthless merchandise to random American consumers. Only in the event of a total rejection will our guidance counselors release the hidden hordes of torch-wielding Union "closers."

We at Severed Oaths feel that, in this way, we can all truly and completely purge ourselves of subconscious violent tendencies, allowing us to focus on our more overt psychotic yearnings. Plus, we can sell some stuff.

Program Leaders: General William T. Sherman & that irritating lady who's fallen and can't get up

Sponsor: Sony of Japan

The Severed Oaths Wall-To-Wall Totally Encompassing And Frighteningly All-Knowing Final And Complete Answer (aka, "Shakra the Monkey")

Led by Shirley Maclaine, Shirley Maclaine (prime), a lady who thought she used to be Shirley Maclaine, the former Shirley Maclaine & Dr. Phil

As we approach seminar's end, you and all the other Severed Oaths' psychic pilgrims will gather for one final ridiculous gesture. Prepare yourself for a journey into Early American Culture as we all enter the sweat Lodge. Within the holy confines of the rich Corinthian Leather teepee, expect to experience all-encompassing visions, one's own unique animal spirit, total peace, and a level of body odor that you cannot imagine.

Here, as we sit on the lap of Gaia, the Mother Earth, we shall all wait the final revelation, a nice maternal dose of Gaia guilt, and your bill. This is a time for slowing down, communal sharing, and reaching for one's temporal wallet. All major credit cards are accepted, and please burn the directions to Severed Oaths before you leave.

SEVERED OATHS: CAST & CREW

Shaman Capote is co-founder of Severed Oaths and calls himself a "self-actualizing life coach," which he says, if you can believe it, with a straight face. After an impressive martial arts career within many of our finer penal institutions, he self-actualized his way over a rather unfriendly fence and began to re-focus on personal pecuniary development. Shaman also doubles as Severed Oaths' Director of Collections and Bad Debts.

Helen Hiwater is co-founder of Severed Oaths and a confirmed but recovering jogger. Always at the forefront of trendy and fleeting national fads, she became entirely transfixed by the lasting influence of ancient meditation therapy, particularly the Kama Sutra, page 115. She will resume instruction of her classes when she returns from the chiropractor.

Roxanne Los Wages came to Severed Oaths four years ago as a very confused little girl and will probably leave just as confused. However, her radical "après-dinner" approach to counselor relaxation techniques has validated her value here at Severed Oaths.

John Smith (a pseudonym), who cautiously wandered into our group one night, has enhanced our instructional staff in the art of surviving off the land, achieving semi-restful states in culverts and spotting plain-clothes policemen. Little is known of his past, and the less we know, the better.

Imotep materialized at Severed Oaths early one evening during a punitive viewing of the film "Ishtar" and has been hovering above the grill hood in the dining room ever since. He spends most of his time in a state of harmonic rapture as watches Jennifer Anniston films over and over again. And he is invaluable as the camp electrician.

Jackson (Big Jake) P. Wellman stumbled into Severed Oaths from deep within the local mountains as he stalked an elusive turkey for Thanksgiving Dinner. Mr. Wellman offers a unique perspective on property rights and is one of the region's leading experts on corn-based beverages. Big Jake runs our Severed Oaths' Real World Readjustment Clinic and is a fine whittler.

Mahatma Blondie, a cybernetic robot, was purchased by our staff as a joke birthday gift from a Upanishads 'R' Us mail-order catalog, during a "buy one, get enlightenment" promotion. However, her inherent ability to predict certain pari-mutuel opportunities involving our equine planetary co-habitants has made her indispensible to our crew. She does, however, exhibit a tendency to short-circuit on "Carbon-Double-Dating Night."

Baba Century Yogi, a former ergonomics coordinator for General Motors, has absolutely no function here at Severed Oaths, but what a name, huh?

Ghin Sue Jones works at the popular Severed Oaths "Endorphins On Demand" clinic as a stress-inducer, utilizing common household items and finely-honed kitchen implements as a source of tension. In her free time, she does extensive volunteer work for "Fathers Without Morals." Primal therapy is her bailiwick. Surprise, surprise.

Itzhak Raoul Headcheese heads up our recruitment program here at Severed Oaths. Armed with only a didactic worldview and a Thompson gun, he has consistently broken all enrollment records, along with nine Commandments and most of our windows. Never, we repeat, NEVER offer this man your "frequent flyer" discounts.

SEVERED OATHS - ARROGANTLY ABSURD

Heroes

(The trick to reality is in learning how to fake it.)

When Parker was younger, the business where he worked consisted of four long double alleys filled with brightly colored boxes. Along the windows and framing the front door and capping the ends of each aisle and back-lighting the back counter were huge, full-color, machine-stamped cardboard cutouts, larger-than-life photos of larger-than-life Modern Heroes.

Technically, the Modern Heroes were just human beings, like Parker and everybody else. But these particular human beings, generally pale-skinned human beings, were born with (or had bought) attractive faces, or strong jaws, or interesting voices, or disciplined chest muscles, or bodies with lots of curves but no hard angles.

The Heroes were all made in a factory on the other side of the country, and Their opinions and actions and lifestyles were made desirable to Parker's customers, thanks to loud noises endlessly generated by the factory. The loud noises were called "Commercials."

Parker would go to work, human beings would come in, stare at one or more colored boxes, and eventually give him money. Money was another loud noise, made in another factory. In exchange for money, Parker would allow the human beings to borrow little black cartridges and take them home.

Inside their uncomplicated houses, the human beings would walk through their growing collection of complicated machines, then insert the little black cartridges into a very complicated machine that would create very believable illusions, full of Modern Heroes.

The Modern Heroes were always doing vile and perfect things in the illusions, and the human beings who watched the illusions would smile, or laugh, or cry, or get very angry, depending on the personal effect each illusion lured out of them.

Meanwhile, in very large houses and jets and bars, the Modern Heroes, Their collective imagination spent by illusion-making, were finding more and more bizarre ways to create Their own illusions. Many of Them would deceive, or damage, or destroy, or die too soon.

The human beings who came in to Parker's store never saw this as stupid. It always seemed romantic to them, because they had to believe it possible that somebody, somewhere, could have a full, rich, romantic, wonderful life.

The little black cartridges were artfully-designed collages of color, and motion, and music, and lots of brisk, short sentences. Spoken sentences, that is: there was very little printed material in any of the illusions, usually only at the beginning, and then again at the ending, when the factory would make lists of all the Modern Heroes, human beings and other machinery involved in creating that particular illusion.

After years of this, even those minimal bits of reading material begin to bore, and the human beings would push buttons on the complicated machine to make the words scroll by very fast and go away, so they wouldn't have to be bothered with reading at all.

After a few more years, schoolteachers even began showing the illusions to their students instead of forcing them to actually *read* a book for a book report.

Sure did.

Sometimes, the human beings would grow so eager and obsessive over the Modern Heroes thrashing out Their illusions that they would steal the brightly colored boxes from the shelves in Parker's store, boxes which didn't even have little black cartridges in them. Parker had learned to remove the actual black cartridges from the boxes on the shelves, shortly after he had learned another sad secret about just how eager and obsessive human beings can be.

And then the human beings would get home and discover that they had not really gotten away with a fistful of free illusions. All they had for company, there at home, in the dark, were empty, pretty boxes.

And lo, the Modern Heroes became highly successful in all types of absurdly unrelated arenas. Reporters would ask Them for Their opinions on world problems or politics or capital punishment or legal precedent or environmental control or the separation of church and state. They had streets named for Them in large and small towns. They were invited to the President's house for dinner, and invited to other countries to complain there about the President here.

Global media outlets spent many dollars and much time trying to discover if the Modern Heroes were privately making bad decisions, and never missed an opportunity to announce any such discoveries, even if they had to create them. And when they couldn't create any discoveries, they created little instant mini-Heroes from real human beings, and set various traps for them, and filmed the human beings falling into the traps, and everybody laughed. This became known as "reality TV."

Sure did.

But the factory that created illusions that Parker swapped for money had been around a lot longer than Parker, or any human beings Parker knew. The factory, therefore, had to create, and constantly recreate, a brand new vocabulary to nudge the human beings into the appropriate emotion for the appropriate illusion. The new vocabulary used words normally associated with destruction and violence, and taught the human beings to get excited by the prospects. So, a very desirable illusion might be called "explosive," "dynamite," or a "blockbuster" or a "big smash hit."

Once, before Parker was born, the factory made illusions called "classics," which meant they contained only two colors, and meant the Heroes had to depend on clever, witty dialogue instead of expensive special-effects, and meant that no human being that Parker knew would ever even remotely consider watching them.

"Special-effects" was the factory's vocabulary word for the practice of showing young children the best possible way to shear off a human being's limbs and destroy a bedroom or an airport at the same time, while simultaneously swearing in three languages and exposing un-sheared-off body parts. The word was later shortened to "Special FX," then shortened again to "SFX." This was another example of the complete linguistic control usurped, over time, by the factory - like describing death in "living color."

Parker received a valuable education in diplomatic tact while assisting the human beings who came in to his store. Many times, concerned mothers would ask Parker to recommend an illusion to show to their impressionable children. The mothers were concerned about the moral content and impact of the illusion. The standard directive was, "Violence is okay, so long as there's no sex in it."

And then there were other remarks, mountainous, eardrum-popping remarks that ascended to altitudes beyond Parker's skills to tactfully navigate.

*** "What's a good movie I ain't seen yet?"

*** "When is this due back? Eight PM? At night?"

*** "Ever watched this one? Ten times, huh? Did you like it?"

*** "I wanna rent a movie, but I got no I.D. with me. Could I just show you my tattoo?"

*** "I heard about this movie, I forget the title, but it's about this man 'n this other guy 'n a train or a boat, and a dog, right? Know the one I mean?"

*** "How much is your free membership?"

And the human beings who came in to Parker's store began to believe that the Modern Heroes were real, that Their lives were real, and that their *own* lives were the illusions. Slowly, over a few factory-dominated generations, human beings began to doubt the significance of their own exist-ence, especially when held up against the perfect, attrac-tive, bite-size, far-away lives of the Modern Heroes.

And greedy steles rose and rose, bricks laid each atop the last, founded on the idea that all good human beings must think just so, talk just so, smell just so, act just so, gratify themselves just so and just so often, and so on, and on.

Sure did.

Heroes, children, like pyramids, are built up, one brick at a time. And, like pyramids, no Hero is really sure how They arrived, or why, or how many innocents were used up in the process. Remember that each brick is placed but once, each atop the last. And remember that each brick is used but once, to build a pyramid, or a bridge, or a wall.

And remember that it's humans who build heroes.

Choose your heroes wisely.

Just Like Home

Dear Cousin,

I wanted to fire off a few words to you, now that I've set up shop here above the South Carolina state line in North Carolina. Believe it or not, things are not so much different here, north of Rock Hill, north of Charleston, south of New York.

I rented a room, first-off, in what might be called a boarding house, allowing me time to look around for a place where I might avoid meeting rabid Baptists. But just like at home, churches brag and apartments hide.

During my first night there, I sat in the kitchen, which doubles as the living room, with three of my new house-mates. They were having beers each, so I thought I ought to join in, and I did, all upbringing to the contrary. Seemed like the polite thing to do.

About an hour later, my new friend Billy, who was drunk, took a playful swipe at my new friend Ralph, who was drunk, and real big. Well, Ralph was not impressed, and he growled a warning to Billy not to touch him. Billy laughed it off and teased Ralph with another playful swipe, and before I saw enough to know to excuse myself, Ralph had leaped up, tackled Billy, and sat on top of him on the pearly linoleum, screaming, "TOUCH ME AGAIN AND YOU'LL NOT WALK RIGHT FOR A WHILE, GREASEBALL!!!"

Well, not yet feeling at home, I took a side - the outside. And then I moved out.

I still haven't yet run into our relatives, who live somewhere close to Raleigh, but people are people - I've met some fine ones and noticed some interesting ones. I imagine (and hope) they're not blood kin. Beer, like at home, is the big daddy here. Canadian Whiskey must be highly taxed here, or something, as it is not offered in a lot of night spots. There's a crime of unusual taxes here.

Concerning fashion, Kelly green is numero uno, and madras shirts also. Just like home. The bartenders, like at home, must be waiting to share some private danger, or danger-ous privacy, with each customer before they'll speak as a friend.

Here in Raleigh, Cousin, I don't feel that rush of stadium fever like we all know from Clemson, even though there are football teams on all sides. Maybe that's *because* there are football teams on all sides. Too many rivals too near to home make claiming a champion dangerous, since glory fades week to week. I guess people hate to be wrong. Just like at home.

Raleigh is a pretty big place, with an obvious fondness for brick. Just down the street from my large, tanned brick office is a large, tanned brick prison. A big boy. Turns out there are four or five prisons in this big city, and this is the city where Sheriff Andy used to take Opie to see a "moving picture show," if Opie had been behaving. Remember that? I guess, with all these handy prisons, Sheriff Andy would bring Opie here if Opie had not been behaving also.

Seems like everyone I've met here is either in school, teaching school or mocking school. I did, however, meet some nice people who were waiting tables and that at a restaurant (now get this) inside the local museum.

This museum is not, like we once joked, a tribute to tobacco products. It's very nice. There is, however, a Jesse Helms wing, in the extreme right wing of the building. Unfortunately, just down the street from the Jesse Helms exhibit is the North Carolina State Veterinary College, and the incredible, nauseating vile stench that wafts over is just awful. Nearly ruins the ambiance of the Vet School.

Cousin, remember all our trips to the hazed-up Blue Ridge Mountains that we used to visit, that seemed to lock Tennessee out of North Carolina? Well, I'm so far removed from that glorious land that we don't get any snow ski reports on the local weather. We get beach conditions and small craft advisories. Too bad. I guess when big city buildings curl up towards heaven, they forget the heaven that curls up the halcyon mountains. Too bad. Just like home.

The state fair has been here for about a week now, and I went in to walk around it last weekend, on a Sunday night. An amazing amount of people was there, and I mean the entire food chain.

I didn't ride any of the flipping, spinning, whirling, heaving, undulating, pitching, tossing rides, since I like to taste my food just once. But the best entertainment at the fair was free. Near the back corner of the "midway," I guess they still call it that, was one of those sad, disappointing ghost mansion deals, where two people get in a car and spend about 2-3 minutes mocking a bunch of poorly-made cloth dummies intended to frighten one to near death. You know the type. Just like at home.

But this one was different. This one had a real person, dressed up in a loose black outfit, with one of those old-man masks on. And this guy was great. He would run in and out of the ride's various doors, hang off the side of the structure, hide in empty cars and that, run up behind cars with jeering kids and moms and couples ("Aw, that weren't nothing!!"), and he would scare the hell out of everybody. Eventually, this guy had a huge crowd standing in front of the ride, tensely holding their breath and waiting for his next attack. People were rolling laughing, and actually applauding from time to time.

When I finally managed to break away to walk on, I turned around and screamed. Standing right next to me was the most horrible nightmare I had ever seen, with this big round bowl of wiry hair, pale skin, big black eyes and blood-red lips, dressed in some kind of drizzly blue coveralls over a garish red baggy shirt. Straight from hell this thing was. But no ... it was somebody's mother. Which was even scarier.

Well, speaking of the fair, it has a place in an interesting story that happened just last night. I went to see a movie at about 7:30 and headed home to my new room at about

9:30. I went by this place near my room to grab a couple of hot dogs — they make the best — and a soda. I appreciate a good dog during late-night reading time.

The place is right next door to this black (I guessed) church, and I mean to tell you that those people got their money's worth, or their souls filled, or whatever the medium of exchange was inside that vibrating hall. The windows to the church were all glazed over so you can't see in, but the "Rev" rocked the block over a microphone and filled the temple with amplified electric promises of better things to come.

I had placed my order and stood leaning against one of the poles when this guy walked up behind me and spoke to me.

"Uh, 'scuse me, man."

"Yeah?"

"I wonder could I get you to order me a sanwich from that man, he woan lemme order nothing, I got the money."

I turned around and looked into the glassed-in kitchen area. The three or four guys working there were pointing and scowling and one walked quickly out the door.

The guy who had spoken to me had large eyes, depressed but alert, settled over a thick black mustache. Pulled down close on his head was a baseball cap with a blue bill, red top, and a white patch on the front on which was stitched "Even Steven" in cursive.

I have no idea what that means.

As I watched, the guy from the kitchen came out and ran off the man with the hat, getting all up in his face, like some white people will do to black people when there is a bunch of white people around and only one black person. I watched the black guy slump away in his blue nylon windbreaker, watched him walk toward the loud church next door.

Meanwhile, my order came up, I paid, turned, walked next door, walked up the steps and opened the door of the church, where the man in the hat had gone.

The sound was deafening. Right inside the door was the man, backing up again, while a huge black woman in a dress way too small was vehemently shaking her head at him and easing him back out the front door of the church. Behind her was a much smaller black woman with a look of fear and disgust on her face.

"Hey!" I yelled out. The guy turned around, looking pretty surprised. "Come on, man," I said to him, holding the door open.

He followed me down the steps of the church, and we turned our backs on all that throbbing Christian grace and mercy.

"Come on, let's find some place for you to eat," I muttered.

"I don't understand it," he complained. We walked to my car. "This one?"

"Yeah, hop in."

The guys in the kitchen were staring and pointing again, looking at me like a traitor or something.

"Man, I walked up here to get a sanwich and asked the man what was the cheapest sanwich you got, you know? And it was about a quarter more'n I had, so I asked this other man for a quarter an' he gave me one, but then the man inside turned me out!"

"Forget 'em," I said.

"I had the money, y'know, an' he woan lemme order nothin'."

"Well," I sighed, "I guess they get a lot of jerks coming in here, bums, lobbyists, Senators and that, you know. I mean, this *is* the State Capitol."

"Yeah, I guess so, but I had the money." He looked at me and stuck out his hand. "William."

I shook his hand as we rode down the street, and told him my name. The hand belonged to a working man. I pulled into a pancake house. "Let's eat, William."

He pointed to the back seat, where I had tossed my hot dogs. "But you already got yours, there."

"It'll keep," I said, parking the car.

"This your car?"

"No, I stole it," I said, but not out loud.

"Yeah," I admitted.

"Looks brand new."

I grinned. "Thanks. Four years old."

"Naah, yeah?"

"Took me a while to get one, so I have to hold on to it for a while, you know?"

"Looks good, man."

We walked in and were seated straight away. All around us were young and old people, Orientals, Blacks, Whites and that, and we were as welcome as any. And this place didn't smell anything like a church.

William ordered a burger and some fries and coffee, which pancake houses brew with a demonic vengeance here. Just at like home. I ordered a side of bacon and no coffee, then proceeded to drink William's. He laughed.

"I thought you ain't want none," he grinned.

"So did I." I asked the waitress for a new cup.

"Did I order too much?" William asked.

"What?"

"Hain't ordered too much, I hope. Y'know."

"Eat," I said, feeling a little uncomfortable, feeling like one of those idiots who go around saying things like 'Well, some of my best friends are black.' I tried to shake it off. "So what are you doing here?"

William slumped down a little, settling a little, molding in to his seat. "I'm from Jacksonville. I worked it up this way north, picking potatoes."

"And you're heading back to Florida now?"

"Uh huh."

"How'd you get up here?"

William stuck out his thumb and grinned. William had a cool grin.

"I wouldn't have thought they grew potatoes in Jacksonville," I thought aloud.

"No," William corrected me. "I'm from Jacksonville, but I came up here to work."

"Oh. Sorry."

William shrugged and looked around the restaurant.

"Well," I continued, "I guess you need to get near Fayetteville or somewhere, get near I-95 to head back to Florida, huh?"

William looked back at me. "Huh?"

"I said I guess you need to get closer to I-95, so you'll maybe have better luck getting south."

William nodded silently. He looked at me, in me, for a few serious seconds. "Man, I 'preciate what you did."

I shrugged. "I've been there."

You know, Cousin, it doesn't take much to be nice to somebody, does it? Just a little human decency.

"What do you do up here?" William asked.

"I'm a writer," I lied.

William dished up another grin. "So you just write stuff down on paper an' there she is, huh?"

"Something like that."

"Well, I got to say thanks again," William went on. "God will take care of you."

I kept my opinions to myself.

"I thought," William ventured, "maybe you ain't live here, neither." He nodded his head toward my car in the parking lot. "You got all those big boxes in the back seat."

I explained briefly to him my situation, still looking for a permanent place and that. William nodded, looked out the window, nodded again.

The food came. Just about 45 seconds later, William looked up at me, wiping off his face.

I smiled. "A little hungry?"

William's laugh was bells ringing a Christmas. "I told you, man, I was starving!"

Suddenly, I had a thought. "You know, William, the fair is in town here, and they're from Florida."

William perked up. "Yeah?"

"Well, I don't know much more than that," I stated, "but they are from Florida, and they've got their own train and that, and maybe you could, you know..."

"Yeah," William pondered. "Maybe, some work ... maybe they..."

"I don't know what their schedule is, you know, I don't know where they're going from here. I can drive you over there."

William looked at me, wide-eyed, as though I'd handed him my wallet or something. "You will?"

"Sure." (And there it came again: 'You know, some of my best friends are black.') "You ready?"

We got up, I paid, we got back in the car. Why did I feel guilty? Or what was it?

We drove through town toward the fairgrounds in silence. The roads were mostly empty, and finally we drove over a hill and saw the lights of the rides. The Fair. Yo.

I don't care where you are or how old you get, I guess you always feel 10 years old and immortal when you see those lights and smell those smells.

"I can take you to that gate, there, William, but that's about all I can do, I guess."

I don't think William even heard me. He was transfixed, staring at the lights, looking at the train, making who knows what kind of plans in his head under that 'Even Steven' cap.

As usual, I drove up the wrong way to the entrance and had to drive right by the fair to turn around.

"You sure you know where you're going?" William grinned.

"Yeah, I need to turn around." I made the turn and pulled up in front of Gate 11.

"Well ..." I said, looking down. I reached in my shirt pocket for a $20 bill I had put there in the restaurant for this purpose. "You'll need five bucks to get in," I said, again confusedly apologetic.

William looked at me and spoke at length about his opinion of me, but he never said a word. He took the bill, looked at it, started to speak, stopped, looked at the bill again. "Whoa. Hain't seen this much money in a long time." He extended his hand one last time.

"Well, hang on to it, then," I fumbled. Damn, Cousin, why did this feel so tough?

We shook hands firmly and William opened the car door. "I don't know, but sometime, man, maybe I can..."

"Yeah, maybe I'll see you around, William. Hang in there."

One more grin from William and I drove away, back to my room to read.

I guess I'll have to find a new place to get hot dogs now, huh?

Write back soon, for I miss you.

Your Cousin

Cue the Stunt Turtle!

(Iran, Toyota, and the FAA compete for the Darwin Awards)

I was getting ready for bed when the first car hit my roof.

I'll have to admit - *that*, I didn't expect. True, it had been an odd week in the news, even by contemporary odd standards. But "a slight chance of cars" in the weather forecast? That's a bit much.

Maybe it happens to you, too. You see something really strange on the news. You count to ten, you blink a few times, you look around, even though you're single and live alone, to confirm. To see if anybody else saw it, too. (Actually, single guys do this more often than you might think.)

So you think, "Okay, give it a minute." And you keep watching, thinking the world can't possibly be this nuts. At least, not consistently.

And then cars start falling on your roof.

The worst part, though, was trying to figure out who was responsible. After a week like this last one, it was difficult to point a finger. There *are* no "usual suspects," because *everything* is unusual.

For starters, there's Iran. Earlier in the week, Iran scoffed off the latest stern threats from the United Nations, including their most harshly-worded warning yet: *"HEY!* Ix-nay on the ombs-bay, or *such* a look we'll give you!" No matter. As usual, Iran's President, McMood Blagojevich, stood on a box and yelled for a while, threatening to vaporize Israel and snuff out capitalism, just as soon as his beard fills in.

Iran then claimed to have test-launched an end-of-life-as-we-know-it missile, bragging that the missile's deadly payload was - and I'm not good enough to make this stuff up - a rat, two turtles and an earthworm.

Great. Now, we're timid in front of a guy that threatens to attack us with three Chinese New Years.

So maybe it was Iran that did the deed to my dormers. Maybe Iran had an out-of-date GPS and attacked my neighborhood, thinking it was the Holy Land, though I don't think we're zoned for that. Maybe they weren't cars at all, but some sort of weird, 4-door Persian turtles.

But many experts doubt Iran's ability to mount such an attack, so some pundits accused Iran of simply filming an entirely made-up event, using computer-generated digital turtles. But that didn't stop the news channels from racing to find the scientist with the most rumpled, slept-in tweed suit, eager to discuss the tactical nuclear yield of your average sand tortoise. The resulting scientific analysis was inconclusive, with expert comments ranging from "total annihilation" to "is this a cash bar?" One wise guy made a bad pun about "shell shock," and was immediately beaten senseless by an exhausted, humorless reporter.

Fox News interviewed one Elgore Snecklin, associate assistant advisor to the assistant associate for the Science Department at the Feast-of-Some-Saints Community College For The Particularly Ungifted, who comfortingly pointed out that the average kill radius of an exploding terrapin is really quite negligible, unless detonated in the upper atmosphere. Snecklin warned that any such high-altitude amphibian ordnance detonation could effectively shut down communication as we know it, which, if Facebook is any indicator, would be no great loss. Fox News promised to blog about it, and suggested that if things go badly, fans could follow the end of the world via one of their Twitter accounts, @Last or #Sand.

So I wasn't at all convinced that Iran was the dastard. Remember: not long ago, an airline passenger from the East, flying to the West, tried to blow up his personal South in the U.S. North. I don't recall if he had a box turtle in his boxers, and I promise to step away from where that joke's going, right now.

Also recall that, last week ... and again, I'm not good enough to make this stuff up ... a 17-foot section of airplane fuselage fell out of the sky into a mall parking lot in Florida, barely missing 26 sexual predators and nearly destroying two bales of cocaine. So maybe somebody's rental car fell out of a plane, ultimately leaving six vinyl siding salesmen from Cleveland stranded on the tarmac in Vegas.

Then, to further complicate my suspect search, we discovered last week that budget cuts had forced NASA to restrict their meteor monitoring to a slice of the heavens approximately the size of Iran's President. So maybe an Acura-shaped asteroid had slipped through the sky-net and scuttled my gutters.

Of course, it's possible that Santa had simply misread my last letter, and mistakenly thought I wanted some "cars." Could be worse. He could have misread it as "scars."

And I'm fairly positive that no American politician was at fault, because I can't think of an American politician clever enough to pull it off. If cars *were* raining on my roof, and politicians did it, then they were likely aiming at something else. On the other hand, fixing my roof *will* save or create millions of jobs.

And at the end of the culpability parade, there's Toyota, who just recalled about 80 million cars after discovering that turning on the car radio may cause some models to erupt into boils, spit acid at Sigourney Weaver, and morph into Godzilla. Other customers have complained that they can't deploy the parking brake without the car breaking down, sobbing uncontrollably and ultimately costing the car's owner a fortune in group therapy. Toyota's marketing department quickly responded by unveiling a new Class-Action-Class sedan, the Toyota "Precedent," which will spontaneously explode in the presence of certain combustibles, like gravel, or air.

So who am I supposed to call? President Obama's not an option - lately, he's gotten so flustered that he recently referred to one branch of the U.S. military as the "Marine Corpse."

And Congress is no help, because it's an election year, rocketing that crowd to a whole new level of Useless. The 2010 Congressional election season (which kicked in about 15 seconds after the 2008 election results were in) is now in high gear, and some members of the club are in deep trouble. For example, one Florida Congressman is being challenged by a dead manatee. And *this* marine corpse is ahead by 8 points.

So. I was on my own. So be it. And I did, finally, manage to get the cars off my house.

But then, just as I was getting ready for bed, Iran exploded a tactical thermo-ninja-turtle device over Detroit.

Priority Male

(The Post Office. The DMV.
The IRS. Meet your new doctors!)

So now I'm dead.

The Department of Motor Vehicles screwed up and swapped a couple of forms. As a result, my driver's license was given a new kidney. But the DMV discovered that my spleen had expired without permission, and they declared me "taxably non-viable."

Great. So now I'm dead.

Of course, I almost never got born in the first place. The "Kilowatts For Kids" incentive program in the Cap & Trade Bill nearly took me out of the world, before I ever even got into the world.

We all saw it coming; we just didn't know how to stop it.

Once "carbon credits" replaced actual US dollars, it was just a matter of time before some Congressional committee saw the literary opening - and ultimately, they did - and "carbon-based life-form credits" became legal tender. And so, one day, a hungry neighbor with an upside-down mortgage ratted out my parents, and my fetus nearly got black-market-swapped for 2 weeks of incandescent lighting tax deferrals. Fortunately, the neighbor was rendered taxably non-viable when a rogue Tea-Party maniac bombed him through the Internet.

Safe! For a while. But my troubles as a 'human wanna-be' were just beginning. It didn't help that I had 'special needs.' My Mom described that dark day.

"Mrs. Johnson, we've reviewed your fetal scan (which is not covered) and found that your child may have special needs (which are not covered), so we must insist that you abort your child (which is not only covered but highly recommended). The procedure is free, but there is an income-level-adjustment fee of $4,000, unless you or your spouse belong to a Federally-designated exempt workers union. Do you need any stamps today?"

Fortunately, my distraught mother bought a roll of ninety-eight-cent stamps, which was such a rare activity that it triggered a computer glitch, causing Cheyenne Mountain to carpet-bomb Ontario, and causing the distracted Post Office clerk to screw up. The on-duty sorter aborted my Dad's monthly edition of "Field & Stream," but somehow, they lost my prognosis, I managed to slip past the Federal goalie, and I got to be born after all.

So I beat the American odds: I survived birth. But that, as it turned out, was just the first hurdle.

When I was 5, I had a very close call. Some bored physician at the IRS back-audited my birth, saw something that didn't look right, and they threw me in a lockbox. However, within a few months, Congress decided to raid the lockbox and use me for something else.

Another hurdle! I was starting to get cocky, in a purely American, post-endometriotic way.

But then, at age 6, during an IRS-mandated "General Brain Function & Schedule C Deductions" examination, they uncovered some more bad news. My IQ was low. The IRS physicians determined this due to my inability to appreciate all of the "rights" that Congress kept granting me. I kept insisting that rights came from God. Whew. No wonder they thought me a mooncalf.

A few years later, after tag, dodge-ball, and the other team sports were outlawed by the Simpatico Czar, I was forced by the Diversity Czar to play lacrosse, in a nod to the ancient cultures who really discovered America. During one particularly intense game, I took a hit in the spleen. The opposing team was immediately whisked off to an Anger Management Gulag. But I didn't qualify for a replacement spleen, since my parents didn't belong to an exempted union.

At the emergency room, I had to wait in line behind some star-struck woman who had just "had dinner next to Angelina Jolie's table," and the poor woman had suffered some kind of "brush with greatness" meltdown. I had a ruptured spleen, but she had pictures of Angelina on her cell-phone, so it took forever for me to get noticed. When I finally got to the front of the line, I was informed, via much pointing and gesturing, that I was in the wrong line. Not my fault. I didn't even know there WAS an "English-only" line.

And so it went. In my case, at least.

I lost the End of Life lottery and couldn't qualify for organ management, because of the organ issue I mentioned earlier. I had no spleen, which was a clear violation of the Health Care Bill, page 62,414, paragraph 9, which requires all patriotic Americans to have more internal organs on the left side of their body. As everyone knows, internal organs on the Left are our friends, while organs on the Right want us to die quickly, and death causes cancer, unless you have a spleen to manage it, which I didn't. Catch-22, American Style.

So now I'm dead. I guess it just wasn't my day. Or year. Or life.

Fortunately, though, my parents have one remaining "Child Allowance" right.

If they can scrape up the stamps.

Season's Gratings

(A Yule blog)

Christmas in America. That special season when our country comes together in a religious ecstasy of inspired shopping. That magical time of year when Catholics remember why they're Catholics, when Methodists remember why they're *not* Catholics, Presbyterians remember why they keep remembering, Jews remember that they forgot to remember, Southern Californians remember why they don't live in Northern Canada, and Baptists remember where the church is.

Secular humanists are getting into the holiday spirit, too, mostly by getting into fights. Christians go to church; humanists go to court. Secular humanists (literal translation: "Followers of Sec") spend a lot of time at tony, upper-East-Side cocktail parties, insisting that all six of them are right, and everybody else is wrong. When they're not suing people, they pony up to buy ads and paste them on public transportation, ads which employ iron-clad debating tactics and bubbly bromides: "No God? No problem!" and "Who needs a god? Just be good for goodness' sake!"

Hard to argue with that logic, especially if your definition of eternity is "grandfathered rent control."

Festive Factoid: Sec, a mythical figure from American Southwest folklore, was the patron saint of Margaritas. He was a large, loud character with three heads and breath that could skin a small goat. According to legend, this three-headed nuisance was often referred to as "Triple Sec."

So here we go again. Christmas in America. Between the bullying and bickering, the whimpering and whining, the apologizing and accommodating, we deck the halls. During dulling "separation of church and state" arguments, we trim the tree. 'Neath festive icicles drips fervent indignation.

I don't know if I'm ready for another season of anti-season protesting. C'mon, America.

In one American town, a disgruntled family removed a tree from a school. The tree wasn't even decorated, for Sec's sake. It was just a tree. Potentially offensive, I guess. Just in case, I suppose. We wouldn't want somebody sneaking in and slinging an ornament on it.

C'mon, America. Christmas is reverent, and relevant, and fun. And Christmas is an integral part of America. Literally. Did you know there's a town called Christmas, Florida? And a Christmas, Kentucky? (There's also a Hell, Michigan, but the Followers of Sec don't believe it exists.)

Festive Factoid: Florida also has a town called Chicken Head. Well, of course it does.

Arizona has both a Christmas and a Humbug, which could go a long way toward explaining John McCain's 2008 campaign strategy. Oklahoma has a North Pole, and scattered across America are cities named Rudolph, Dasher, Vixen, Comet, Cupid, Donner and Blitzen. Dancer and Prancer were once cities, too, but they were caught crafting a Christmas crèche, so those towns were run out of town.

In cities all across America, Christmas affects people, one way or another. Recently, in an Atlanta mall, a 40-year-old man dressed as an elf triggered a commerce-interrupting panic when he told the mall Santa that he had a bag full of dynamite. Even more odd, the 40-year-old was sitting on Santa's lap at the time. Santa was hauled in for questioning by Child Protection Services.

Festive Factoid: Speaking of cities, I understand there's a Wiseman in Arkansas. (Recent Arkansas political history notwithstanding)

And nobody decorates for Christmas like us Americans, even the Michiganites in suburban Hell. Right here in my neighborhood, there's an 8-foot-tall, inflatable Santa Claus. Fine. But this Santa has a transparent tummy, and inside Santa's belly is a small grinning Nordic mammal. That's just wrong.

Another context-challenged, nog-inspired neighbor has deployed every single lawn ornament ever created. Driving by, one sees Santa and Seuss' Grinch, angels and gnomes, carolers and confused antebellum archetypes. Over here is the entire cast of 'Bambi.' Over there are three overdressed Wise Men, chatting up Snow White. Reindeer root around in the Bethlehem manger, antler-to-snout with Porky the Pig. Nearby, a shepherd lies prone on the lawn, possibly imbued during an over-zealous Margarita ritual. And I still don't get the connection between Christmas and the seven Disney dwarves.

The economy's not helping, either. A few days ago, our President personally threw the switch to light the capitol's Christmas tree and then declared, "It works!" Gape-jawed throngs fell to their knees in front of the miracle, including 5 of the 6 humanists. And once word got out that the tree had a job, 10 million unemployed Americans rushed to have themselves reclassified as "hardwood."

Santa's elves (North Pole Local #26) struck for overtime wages and refused to wrap another gift until they were guaranteed Universal Elf Care.

Festive Factoid: Not long back, Nancy Pelosi, who smiles so much that I wonder about her limbic system, declared Universal Health Care a "Christmas present for America." This caused three locals from Wiseman, Oklahoma, to start following a star. But it wasn't a star; a galactic Unmitigated-Gall-O-Meter had simply overloaded, and it blew up.

And just last week, economists calculated that it would cost $87,403 (in 2009 dollars) to buy all the gifts enumerated in "The Twelve Days of <Censored>mas," if America still had any dollars.

And speaking of pipers piping: I love Christmas music, even when stores start piping it at us before Labor Day. But it can get out of hand. Earlier this week, I heard REO Speedwagon doing a cover of "Silent Night." That's just wrong. I wanted to throw a penalty flag, but the University of Georgia Bulldogs football team had already used up all the penalties in the known universe.

REO Speedwagon singing "Silent Night." That's like Sinatra, in punk boots, spandex pants and an open Hawaiian shirt, shoo-be-doo-ing his way through the Rolling Stones' "Can't You Hear Me Knocking." A thing like that could put you right off the egg nog.

Festive Factoid: Congress issued an injunction against Santa Claus, insisting the jolly fellow use green-friendly energy instead of coal. In an unrelated story involving a neighborhood watch group in Chicken Head, Florida, Frosty the Snowman was hauled in for questioning by Child Protection Services.

And when I got home today, I found that the Followers of Sec had cut down all the trees in my yard.

Just in case.

Merry Ethno-Generic Fully Optional Deity-Nonspecific Seasonal Timespan!

Gravity and Andy

(One small man, one large universe,
one lousy afternoon for both)

Andy shifted on the low-pitched couch as he closed the thick paperback. Seven hundred pages in three days was pretty remarkable for his manic work schedule, but this had been A BOOK … it had simply kidnapped him. He dropped the fat thing behind the ashtray on the end-table. He yawned and began to stretch.

His arms slowly creaked toward the sky, canting outwards at off-center angles like the crippled arms of some junk-yard clock. His shoulders wriggled upwards one at a time, as if to deny Gravity, as if to talk the tension into sliding down and off his back. At the apogee of his stretch, his fingers spread and contracted, extracting Lilliputian creaks.

All these pops and snaps began to irritate Gravity.

-~-~-~-~-~-

Leaving his right hand up, Andy retracted his left hand and planted it across his left cheek, just slightly pressing into that bracelet of bone that protected his eye. He rubbed, tentatively, as if trying to locate an elusive switch.

Gravity sneered and grabbed a beer.

-~-~-~-~-~-

Andy slid that hand down and across his face, coming to rest at the terminal of his neck. There he clasped the fingers of his right hand in an inverted perversion of the "Praying Hands" that rode atop so many TV consoles in his past. Ten fingers met and joined, creaking and popping in delicious readjustment.

Gravity began to get an idea, and a grin broke out on Its face.

-~-~-~-~-~-

Andy's eyes rolled back in his head like a shark's eyes, and he held this pose religiously for a few seconds. Then he snapped his head forward and slung his hands down, smacking the tops of his thighs. He hunched forward and rose, like a crusty rusted car jack, pushing himself out of the couch, which answered with creaks of its own.

Gravity, muttering, opened another beer.

-~-~-~-~-~-

Once erect, Andy clenched his fists and drove them forward and beyond each other, locking himself in an intense embrace with no one. Andy grabbed his shoulders and twisted violently left, then right, calling up cackles from the flat bones up and down his back.

Gravity, feeling the beers, began humming a little tune, something It had overheard in Pisa, Italy.

-~-~-~-~-~-

Andy drew in his breath and leaned forward from the hips, his arms loosely waving above the ground. He hung there, unmoving.

Gravity watched this seemingly unwound robot, arms waving as if in some unseen wind. Gravity belched.

-~-~-~-~-~-

After some time, Andy, the reviving machine, lurched upright and concluded his ritual. He placed his left hand in his back pocket and with his right, adjusted his crotch with all the intimacy of an Italian waiter.

Gravity, anticipating, rubbed Its hands together and flicked a well-used switch.

-~-~-~-~-~-

Now fully alert, Andy began to walk toward the counter and back to business. He paused slightly to stoop to his right and pry the paperback off the syrupy surface of the coffee-stained table.

Gravity licked Its lips.

-~-~-~-~-~-

This slight off-centered stooping caused Andy's knee to pop audibly. Grimacing, he dropped his left hand in a protective grip.

Gravity grinned.

-~-~-~-~-~-

In the close space between the wall and the counter, Andy's rapidly dropping left shoulder met the firm wooden corner of the counter, causing him to dribble the book onto the floor at his feet. Lurching away from the counter, his foot caught in the carpet where it had been laterally cut to allow for "safe" routing of the cords to his electric piano.

Completely out of control, Andy stumbled and fell forward.

Gravity's eyes bulged and beer exploded from Its mouth in a desperate attempt to get out of the way of an erupting laugh.

-~-~-~-~-~-

A noise like a chubby man choking escaped Andy's surprised face as he tumbled forward into the edge of the piano, upending a two-day-old glass of whiskey and a sheath of papers which hid an insanely filled ashtray.

Andy's next mistake was an explosive eviction of air, unfortunately in the proximity of the newly-fermented and migrating cigarette ashes. They spewed skyward in a matted scuddy cloud. A mawkish and adhesive gray pate' found his eyes, his nose, his mouth, and stuck like dusky rouge to his cheeks.

Gravity, moaning in glee, made a mental note to cancel Its cable subscription, considering that It could watch stuff like this for free.

-~-~-~-~-~-

Grasping blindly, Andy's right hand wildly arced, finally gripping the smooth surface of a two-inch dowel. The dowel ran six feet straight up from the carpet to sustain an 80-pound speaker, which Andy had decided sounded much better from up there.

Gravity watched, knowing full well that pulling on a dowel will loosen any lone nail that holds it onto a speaker's shelf.

Then Gravity took over.

-~-~-~-~-~-

Eighty pounds of horrid reality caromed off the wall and erupted in loud shudders of destruction, taking up residence within the guts of the piano cabinet. The poor Fender keyboard shrieked out a discordant death-knell at the intrusive speaker, which tilted crazily upwards, still belting out Oscar Peterson's jazz riffs.

Gravity, like Physics, hates jazz.

-~-~-~-~-~-

The sound of the collision sent Andy shooting backwards and away from the soul-wrenching clamor.

Gravity reached over and set Its VCR on 'RECORD.' It popped another beer.

-~-~-~-~-~-

Muttering and rubbing his eyes and spitting out little remnants of ash cocktail, Andy landed his foot squarely on the now-damp cover of that wonderful paperback, and he skated in reverse toward a large planter next to the couch. When his elbow hit the stout trunk of the plant, he spun to his left, slamming his hip into that seemingly omnipresent counter-top corner.

Gravity clutched Its side in a painful stitch of laughter.

-~-~-~-~-~-

Clutching wildly at his own side, Andy pounced backward like a threatened cat and hit the back of his knees against the end-table.

Gravity howled.

-~-~-~-~-~-

Andy's feet shot into the air, the paperback still glued to his foot. Over the sloppy surface of the table slid this now highly animated "robot," his butt like a broom, sweeping piles of magazines, near-empty cigarette packs, disposable lighters and a phone into the folds of the couch.

Gravity hooted and opened another beer.

-~-~-~-~-~-

Falling backwards, lengthwise, across both cushions, Andy's legs were again propelled skyward, freeing the soot-covered paperback to arc with a plop into his lap.

A cloud of noxious smells circled and settled in and around Andy's collapsing universe, like illusory snowfall swirling inside a small mantle-top Christmas decoration; just a tiny human locked in a seamless glass bubble's blizzard of olfactory dandruff.

Gravity reached for the phone.

-~-~-~-~-~-

Andy, stunned, lay very still.

As he attempted to regain some shard of motor and sensory control, his compact disc player, having by now collected a fair-sized set of settling cigarette ashes, began to repeat a single note, repeating and repeating and repeating.

Gravity, snickering, thanked Inertia and hung up the phone.

-~-~-~-~-~-

Andy sighed. Sitting on the damp couch, he stared at the damp paperback in his damp lap. His eyes slowly began to narrow. Then, deliberately, Andy got up, grabbed the fat thing and fished a lighter out of the couch. He headed for the fireplace, his lips slightly curled in a tight grin of pure purpose.

Andy never read another book again.

-~-~-~-~-~-

"Merry Christmas," sneered Gravity. Chuckling, It put the small Christmas decoration back on Its mantle and watched the illusory snowfall settle. Feeling very pleased with Itself, Gravity reached up and It began to stretch, Its arms slowly creaking toward the sky, canting outwards at off-center angles like the crippled arms of some junkyard clock...

-~-~-~-~-~-

Reigning Cats & Dogs

(Comments from the top of the
food chain, while I'm still up here.)

Good grief. It was already a rough week. And now I owe my cat two million bucks.

Don't laugh! And don't think it can't happen to you! Thanks to some of society's far-point fringe elements, pets can now sue their "owners." My cat lawyered up, bought a stylish but modest business ensemble, sued me, and won.

I'm not sure exactly when animals managed to gain more human rights than humans, but it's nearly a done thing. Prodded by "progressive" policies from PETA, the Animal Liberation Front, the Animal Rights Militia, Oz's winged monkeys, and other seriously under-medicated entities, domestic pets and their more feral cousins are very close to flipping the Garden of Eden gig and taking dominion over man (if we can still say "man").

According to my exhaustive research, performed while watching my cat's lawyer swim by in a Shark Week documentary, Americans collectively spend some 200 conskillion dollars each year on pet care, over ten times more than we spend on books, and if you rule out books that don't discuss diets, the total drops to about a dollar-fifty. Animal nurturers can buy gourmet pet food, invest in memory-foam beds, send their pets off to summer camp, look into kennel career counseling and donate to causes like "Winged Monkeys Are People, Too."

Political correctness now applies to the animal kingdom, too. You mustn't say "black sheep" or "white whale" or "red herring" or "dark horse." You can't call someone "crazy as a loon" or "blind as a bat" or "fat as a pig." You can still lead a horse to water, but you shouldn't want to be *making* the horse drink in the first place, you vile biped, you. You snake in the grass. You cold duck.

And I won't even bring up "Whack-A-Mole." Or "bitch."

Now, these anthropomorphic activists may have a point. Last Christmas (if we can still say "Christmas"), I was given a bird feeder, and it's become a huge hit, bird-wise. A bright red Cardinal flew by and blessed the food, and an excommunicated squirrel blessed out the Cardinal. But I've been monitoring all the avian activity, and apparently I'm infested with Congressional birds. They strut and preen, bicker amongst themselves, complain about a seemingly endless supply of food that they didn't pay for (but act like they deserve), leave a huge mess, all with nary a nod of thanks.

They also freely decorate my deck with ... well, let's call them "mementos." You know, the airborne version of rab-bit pellets. The animal kingdom's equivalent of Congressional sound bites.

Of course, it could be worse. They could be Progressive birds. They could spend the day handing out little bird manifestos, snidely looking down their beaks at the rest of us, demanding we put bird seed in our neighbors' feeders.

All over America, protected species have gotten so over-protected that they're over-procreating, and eating up other species, who were just running around minding their own business, procreating, and occasionally morphing into Darwinian finches. As a result, these innocent animals are now the new endangered species, taking their own turn at guest-starring on stamps, billboards, and celebrity outrage-a-thons.

By the way: speaking of procreation - and it's about time somebody did - thanks to dedicated (albeit misguided) scientific research, we now know that timing can be really critical to ensure the successful mating of pandas.

Whew. As a satirist, I *live* for news like this.

First, the human bad news. Somewhere out there is a zoo intern nursing a stopwatch, a biorhythms chart, and a foul attitude about his career decision. And then there's poor Andy Panda, rehearsing his best panda pick-up lines while bitterly staring at the sulking undergrad, who's looming there with a clipboard at the foot of the conjugal panda memory-foam bed. "Hey, Stopwatch Boy! Buzz off! I'm try-ing to bust a move over here!"

In other science news, studies claim to prove that coffee can control Alzheimer's in mice, and I'd pay good money to learn how they test *that*. Maybe they give out little Star-bucks discount cards for Christmice, then administer a TSA security guard exam and see if the mice pass or fail (if we can still say "fail").

Other scientists have discovered that dogs are not only smart; as a defense mechanism, dogs will sometimes actively hide their intelligence from nearby humans. I've often suspected the same thing of network executives, and government workers (if, in that context, we can still say "work"). And unlike some high-level government employees, most dogs can at least handle TurboTax.

And now the winged monkeys have formed a political action committee, hired a spokes-simian, and moved to Nebraska. As a result, the other 49 states will be forced to pay for their anger management therapy.

But anyway, my cat and her lawyer, a junior partner at the law firm of Spawn, Spawn & Legion, sued me for irreconcilable differences, or, as the cat spelled it, x.

Don't blame the cat. Remember, to err is animal.

Maybe I was convicted for not garnishing her cat food with a sprig of parsley. And maybe you think I'll gracefully accept the verdict and simply write the brat cat a big check.

In a pig's eye.

High Noon in Debt Valley

(This may be the first White House to win an Oscar)

The harsh sun beat down on the low desert. Nearby, a high-horse snorted, and somewhere, a blue-dog barked. Two sand-whipped saloon doors grudgingly creaked open, and eight stock actors dressed as cowboys filed out. They clattered on to the porch and hit their marks.

Next door to the saloon, in a unique high-backed rocker, sat an odd and oddly-grinning woman. It was Dotty Speaker, the Madame at that accommodating parlor known as the People's House. Dotty rocked left, then farther left, then back to the left again, taking it all in, slowly twirling the talon-scarred gavel she wore round her neck. Behind her, 434 prostitutes peered out through the windows of the People's House, endlessly jostling each other for visibility.

The saloon doors swung wide once more, and out stepped the new Sheriff.

Klieg lights blazed and spotlights sheared in, wrapping the attractive leader in a corona of confidence. Switches were flicked, and the easy, loping music of a fiddle filled the dusty street. The Sheriff positioned himself midway between two tactical tumbleweeds.

Dotty leapt to her feet and applauded. The Sheriff looked her way and touched the brim of his hat.

"Madame Speaker."

The Sheriff then nodded to the Mayor, Harry Screed, and his sidekick, Cap'n Trade. Out of sight, a guitar was strummed, slowly, just once.

Right on cue, a muddied scream spilled into the street from the town's troubled bank, the Beltway Gulch Imaginary Savings & Eventual Loan. Debt Valley's mortally-bloated addict, Fannie Mae, waddled out the bank's door, pitiful and terrified, howling for her very life. Close on her heels came that dastard, Billy Wrights, guaranteed-access guns blazing. Smoldering shreds of ACLU position papers peppered his thick beard.

All eight prop cowboys simultaneously reached for their holsters, but the Sheriff calmly raised his hand, coolly shook his head.

Fannie Mae managed to make the street. She staggered across and crumpled, clinging to the Sheriff's leg, carefully avoiding his chronic tendinitis. Billy stepped out of the bank's long shadow and eased to the right, his trigger finger twitching.

The Sheriff's eyes narrowed. An audio tech nudged a knob, and the mournful fiddle was joined by the slow heartbeat of a tympani.

"Still here, are ya," grinned Billy. "Well, I don't reckon Debt Valley's big enough for the both of us."

Blush

The Sheriff ripped off his nicotine patch and ground it out with his free foot. In a flash, he whipped out several ink pens and a piece of parchment, scribbled his name one letter at a time, and Billy Wrights vanished in a hail of regulation and diverted funds.

Linseed Graham, the town barber, was furious. "Hey! That ain't right! He never stood a chance!"

"Nope," drawled the Sheriff, reading from a tumbleweed. "He weren't never meant to."

"See?" Screed poked Cap'n Trade. "Accent or no accent. Like a faucet."

The Sheriff stepped up to a small cactus, adjusted the volume, and then began to speak:

"It's great to virtually be here. Before I get started, I wanna recognize a few faces in the crowd. I see our local party co-chairs, Juan and Janet Evening. Y'all know them. Nobody's worked harder on this bill than Juan and Janet."

All eight cowboys grinned and clapped. Dotty Speaker blew Juan a kiss, but her elbow got caught in her teeth.

"And I understand your Governor, Mike Offers, is in the house. Where's Mike? Nobody's worked harder on this bill than Mike," read the Sheriff. "Y'all give it up for Mike Offers. Pause knowingly. Raise chin. And way in the ba...oops."

Two of the less bright prop cowboys raised their chins. One tried to pause knowingly.

"And way in the back, there's my buddy, cattle rancher Needham Swettin. Needham hasn't worked a lick on this bill - heck, Needham's the kinda guy who wouldn't cross the street to spit on a man who was on fire. But he's got *sacks* of money, and we're all hopin' he'll make a nice contribution to Mike Offers."

Screed's eyes lit up. He pulled out some comp plane tickets and sidled over towards Mike.

The Sheriff switched tumbleweeds and subtly adjusted his pose.

"Okay. Let's talk seriously about our cattle problem. Here in my hand, I have a let...here in my hand, I have a let...here in my hand, I have a let..."

A crouched technician spidered on to the street, jiggled one of the tumbleweeds, and dashed off.

"Here in my hand, I have a letter from a rancher who lost all his cattle to a low-down rustler. The rancher's insurance company refused to reimburse him, claiming the rustler's low-down-ed-ness was a pre-existing condition."

The Sheriff paused, allowing the street to see his profile. He checked the tumbleweed, squinted, and then continued:

"Now, according to polls, we got millions of cows, right here in America, although 14% of those polled have no opinion. And each cow has several legs. Cows have had multiple legs ever since Al Gore invented cows. And as you can see, there are real cowboys standing behind me, who all agree that we got tons of cows, and almost every one of 'em's got four legs. These aren't just my numbers."

On cue, the cowboys collectively thumb-groomed their moustaches and scratched themselves, in a bipartisan, colloquial, cowboy-like way.

The Sheriff stretched out his arms.

"Now, I didn't want to do this. I inherited this mess. True, I inherited the mess a really long time ago, but forget that - just stare at my profile and look at my outstretched arms. Make no mistake. We have to act, and we have to act now. We have a serious crisis that has saved or created millions of speeches."

"Zoom and rack," whispered the director. "Cue the chorus!"

The Sheriff raised his arms.

"Doing nothing is not an option. And it's too late to start over, 'cause all over America, as I've always said, cows already have feet. There are just too many cows, with too many feet. And that's why *we will pass Universal Hoof Care this year.* Thank you, and I bless America."

Madame Speaker leapt to her feet, begging for an ink pen. The cowboys broke into wild synchronized applause, except for one who was texting his agent. Arm in arm, Screed and Mike slipped into the bank. Across the land, the light dimmed in America.

And the Sheriff rode off as the Bush tax cuts began to sunset.

Made in the USA
Charleston, SC
13 October 2010